deadly PINK

deadly pink

Vivian Vande Velde

Harcourt

Houghton Mifflin Harcourt   Boston   New York   2012

Harcourt is an imprint of
Houghton Mifflin Harcourt Publishing Company.
www.hmhbooks.com

Text set in 11-pt. Berling LT Std

Library of Congress Cataloging-in-Publication Data
Vande Velde, Vivian.
Deadly pink / by Vivian Vande Velde.
p. cm.
Companion book to: Heir apparent and User unfriendly.
Summary: Fourteen-year-old Grace must find a way to get her older sister out
of a princess-filled virtual reality RPG (role playing game)—before it is too late.
ISBN 978-0-547-73850-5
[1. Fantasy games—Fiction. 2. Role playing—Fiction. 3. Virtual reality—Fiction.
4. Computer games—Fiction. 5. Sisters—Fiction. 6. Science fiction.] I. Title.
PZ7.V3986De 2012
[Fic]—dc23
2011027324

Manufactured in the United States of America
DOC 10 9 8 7 6 5 4 3 2 1
4500358846

To Marianne—like a sister,
only without the fighting over closet space
and borrowed makeup

contents

CHAPTER 1

The Dangers of Higher Education

MY MOTHER isn't normally the kind of parent who comes to school and has me yanked out of class because she needs to see me.

Never mind that the class I was pulled from was trigonometry, which is monumentally mind-numbing and—as far as I can tell—entirely useless to anyone except trigonometry teachers. It is rumored that, on a warm spring day three years ago, our trig teacher, Mr. Petersen, actually fell asleep during one of his own lectures. The speculation is that he has not awakened since, but is still droning on from memory, in a sleepwalking state.

I have never seen anything in Mr. Petersen's demeanor to make me doubt that rumor.

Generally speaking, I'd be eager for *any* excuse to get away from sine and cosine and whatever that third function is whose name I can never remember. But I felt a prickle of anxiety. Despite my mother's inability to come up with even one real-life situation where knowing the difference between opposite and adjacent, much less a hypotenuse would be a benefit to me, she does strongly believe in the theory of education. So I couldn't make sense of the note the messenger from the office interrupted the class to hand to me:

Grace Pizzelli
Go down to Mrs. Overstreet's
office right away.
Your mother is here

My brain instantly zipped to the West Coast, where Dad was attending a sales conference at a hotel I was suddenly convinced was the obvious target for arsonists, kidnappers, earthquakes, flash floods, outbreaks of Lyme disease, and/or killer bees.

My outlook wasn't improved by walking into Mrs. Overstreet's office. Mrs. Overstreet was wearing that I-smell-something-bad-and-I-suspect-it's-coming-from-you expression that must be taught in one of the required courses at principal college—a course that clearly would be more useful than trig.

But my mother had on sweatpants and a Milky Way Galaxy T-shirt she'd gotten when she'd chaperoned my Brownie troop's overnight at the Strasenberg Planetarium seven years ago. This is strictly at-home wear for her. Even for going to the grocery store, Mom's shoes need to match her purse. On this particular occasion, her shoes didn't match each other.

My prickly-all-over worry exploded into panic. "What's wrong? What's happened?" I asked. "Is Dad all right?"

My questions seemed to send my mother into a worse spiral than she was already in. "Dad?" she echoed. She glanced around the office, looking simultaneously dazed and frantic, as though not sure whether to level accusations at Mrs. Overstreet or the two strangers in the room—a man and a woman. She settled on the strangers and said in a squeaky voice, "You didn't tell me something happened to my husband!"

The man had a trim little beard, and—excuse me, but if you were a casting director looking for someone to play the role of a debonair devil, you'd be giving this guy your card and asking him to come in for an audition. By contrast, the woman might well have been studying for that principal's course on intimidation through facial expression, but she was the one who spoke: "Mrs. Pizzelli, we don't even know where your husband is."

Mom's voice went even higher. "Tyler is *missing?*"

My feelings were bouncing all over the place because I didn't know if Mom was overreacting—which has been known to happen—or if she actually had a reason to suspect the worst.

Mrs. Overstreet went with option number one. "Mrs. Pizzelli, I'm sure your husband is fine." She didn't give my mother a chance to say more than "But—" before she continued, "When I go to conferences, the presenters always ask everyone to turn off their phones. I'm sure once they break for lunch, your husband will check his messages and return your call."

The other woman was nodding as though those were her thoughts exactly. "Please," she said, "now that your younger daughter is here, let's talk about Emily."

Emily?

Before I could ask "What's wrong with Emily?" the woman had stood up and offered me her hand to shake. She was very business-chic and sophisticated. "Hello, Grace. I'm pleased to meet you. Though not under these circumstances, of course."

The man, still sitting, smoothly interjected: "By which we do not mean to imply that Rasmussem Corporation or any of its employees is in any way responsible for those circumstances."

Ah, I thought, putting together that suave but slightly sinister look with his precise wording. *Lawyer.*

I finally noticed that they both had Rasmussem Corporation nametags, as well as school visitor badges.

The woman continued, "My name is Jenna Bennett, and I'm the chief technical engineer at the Lake Avenue Rasmussem facility. This is Alexander Kroll, from our legal department."

Mr. Kroll showed some of his teeth and added, "By which we do not mean to imply that this is a matter requiring adjudication."

Apparently, my principal didn't like lawyers. She leveled an I-am-picturing-doing-you-bodily-harm expression at him and said to my mother, "Yeah, yeah, so it's much too early to talk about suing the pants off them, but that's always a possibility."

Kroll's expression didn't change: proof, if anyone had needed it, about the sincerity of his smile.

Suing didn't sound good. People sue when something goes terribly wrong, and what did all this have to do with Emily—or me?

Ms. Really-I'm-an-Engineer-Despite-the-Fact-That-I-Look-Like-a-Principal-in-Training Bennett put on a pained expression.

But, fashionable and pretty as she was, she didn't know *pained*. My mother's eyes were red-rimmed and scared—*that* was pain. She took my hand and worked it like someone trying to soften up putty.

What a terrible person I am, I realized. *Something awful has happened to Emily, and here I am mentally moaning about a few squished fingers.*

Mom said to me, "Emily's playing a game at the arcade."

"Okay . . ." I said, knowing there had to be more. Emily

is a student at RIT—Rochester Institute of Technology. She's studying technical engineering and is in a work co-op program at Rasmussem, which, long story short, means she's slave labor for them this semester, though I'm guessing Mr. Lawyer Kroll would try to qualify that statement. Rasmussem is the company that developed total immersion, the next step beyond virtual reality. When you play their games, sensations are fed directly into your brain: you can feel the warmth of the sun if it's daytime in the world you're playing in, just as you can feel cold and soaked to the bone if it's raining; you can taste the food and smell the flowers; and if you're riding a horse, after a while your butt goes to sleep. The difference between playing a Rasmussem game and a regular old virtual reality game is like the difference between watching an IMAX movie and one of those old black and white silent films.

I thought, *Of course Emily is playing games at the arcade.* No doubt most—if not all—of the people who work at Rasmussem are there because they love games. Well, maybe excepting the lawyers. But if the company wasn't going to pay their interns salaries, they couldn't be surprised at an unauthorized game or two. I assumed Emily was playing while she was supposed to be working, which apparently I didn't take as seriously as the legal department did. Was she getting fired? Was she getting expelled?

But surely that wasn't enough to account for Mom's distress, or for my getting called out of class.

Mom still seemed intent on kneading all my fingers into mush. She said, "They can't get it to stop."

Confused, I said, "The games last a half-hour. While you're playing, you feel like it's hours, but it's only thirty minutes." I figured my mother wasn't sure whether to believe me. She's not a gamer—hard as that is to conceive of these days. She's not into technology and can barely get her phone to cooperate. I said, "When the time runs out, the game just stops."

"Yes," Ms. Rasmussem-Engineer-Lady agreed. "Normally."

Okay, well, granted, something was not normal or we wouldn't all be here.

She continued, "Emily hooked herself into the game she was developing, and . . . she did something. She bypassed safety protocols. But the half-hour is up. The half-hour was up more than four hours ago."

"Can't you just . . ." Of course I *have* played Rasmussem's games, but Emily is the tech-type in the family. ". . . unhook her?" I finished lamely, thinking of the wires they stick to your head when you lie down on a total immersion couch. Duh. Like the people who could think up total immersion weren't smart enough to think of that?

"We did," Ms. Bennett said, without sounding impatient or condescending at my obviousness. "She didn't revive."

Mom said, "I asked them to just pull the plug on the whole thing, but they won't." Pulling the plug is Mom's cure-it technique for *all* of our computer's ills.

Ms. Bennett said—and I could tell she'd said it before— "It doesn't work like that."

"There should be safeguards," Mom said.

"There are," Mr. Kroll told her. "Your older daughter, intentionally, with forethought, for her own reasons, disabled them. Leaving behind a note clearly showing her culpability."

From his briefcase, he pulled out a piece of paper in a clear plastic bag hand-labeled EVIDENCE.

Evidence? Like from courts and trials and cop shows? What sort of trouble was Emily in?

The note was in my sister's neat rounded penmanship. It said:

Not anybody's fault.
This is MY choice.

While the word *evidence* had set off all sorts of alarm bells in my head, now I think my body temperature dropped ten degrees.

Emily had *chosen* to go into a game and not come out? *Why?*

Mr. Kroll was still talking to my mother. "There may

well be loss to company revenues because of her actions, beyond the time of the techs who have been trying to help her, beyond the time taken by Ms. Bennett and myself to explain things to you at your home, and now here again at your younger daughter's school because you wanted to consult with her." His expression clearly showed what he thought of a woman who would seek her fourteen-year-old's opinion.

"Be that as it may . . ." Principal Overstreet said.

We all looked at her, but she didn't really have anything to say; I guess she just didn't like our bickering.

Ms. Bennett stepped into the breach, too elegant to put up with bickering, either. "Be that as it may, we can tell, approximately, where in the Rasmussem-created scenario she is. I myself went in and tried to talk her out. She refused to listen to me."

This was so weird, so . . . *more* than weird. I couldn't even tell what I should be thinking.

I saw Ms. Bennett looking at me, waiting for me to realize she was looking at me. She said, "We're hoping she'll listen to you."

Me? Somehow this was coming down to *me*?

I had caught that part where Ms. Oh-So-Well-Dressed Bennett had said she'd *gone in* to talk to Emily.

"I think it's insane," Mom said. "First one of my daughters gets stuck in their crazy game; then they want my other daughter to just step right in after her."

"Mrs. Pizzelli," Ms. Bennett said, "I've already explained: there's no danger. I told you that I went into the game and was perfectly capable of coming back out again. Emily could come out, too. She's simply choosing not to. We're hoping Grace can get her to see reason."

Liking a game is one thing. Playing into the wee hours of the morning even though it's a school day is one thing. Shouting "Just a minute" when your mother hollers at you to get off the computer *now* because she's called you for dinner twice already—all of that is one thing.

Emily wouldn't come out?

"If," Mom said, "*if* someone from the family needs to do this, it should be me."

Ms. Bennett shook her head. "You're not a gamer. You'd be overwhelmed. Without experience, you wouldn't know where to begin, how to get around, what's important and what's only background. We'd lose valuable time. The programs are meant to last from thirty to sixty minutes. The equipment is rated safe for eight times that exposure. But it's not meant for sustained immersion."

Everything she said made sense, too much sense. There was no way I could hope Mom would insist on being the one to go—not when I could see so clearly it would be better for Emily to have me there.

In the movies, the good guys always fight each other for the opportunity to do the dangerous stuff. The Rasmussem people were saying this *wasn't* dangerous. And *still* the responsibility was enough to freeze me solid.

Mrs. Overstreet, as a principal in charge of her students' safety, said to me, "Grace, you don't have to do this if you don't want to."

For the first time in my life, I wanted to hug her.

"No," Ms. Bennett agreed. "Of course she doesn't *have to*. But there's no reason she shouldn't. It's not like we're asking her to donate a kidney or something."

Suddenly we were into donating body parts? *Would* I donate a kidney? I wondered. Much as I loved Emily, I wasn't sure I could.

"Oh, I wish your father would pick up the damn phone," Mom said, "and tell me what we should do."

Somehow, that cleared my head. *We SHOULD*, I thought, *be able to make up our minds on our own*.

"No danger of me getting stuck in there?" I asked.

"Absolutely none," Ms. Engineer and Mr. Lawyer said in unison.

"Then," I had to admit, "I guess I don't see any reason why not."

My mother sniffled but didn't try to talk me out of it.

Mr. Kroll smiled his non-smile smile and opened his briefcase again. "Fine. We just have one or two papers for you to sign . . ."

CHAPTER 2

The Other Sister

THE RASMUSSEM PEOPLE had a mobot, one of those new artificial intelligence cars—the kind you program, and don't need a driver for. I've been in one a few times, because the Arnold family has one, and Mrs. Arnold has chaperoned a couple of our class field trips. My mother, of course, doesn't trust the technology. Although she admits that computers can react faster than humans in most cases, she keeps thinking some sort of situation will arise that the computer hasn't been programmed for, that a human driver could think his or her way around. Mr. Kroll pointed out to her that there hasn't been a single accident involving a city bus ever since they switched over to artificial intelligence drivers.

"The buses have robotic drivers," Mom argued as we all climbed into the mobot limo. The limo looked odd, like a toy, because the whole vehicle was like the *back* of a limo— just seats for riders, no front seat or steering wheel or anything.

"The robotic driver is just to give people something to look at," Mr. Kroll said. "The technology is the same. Once people get sophisticated enough to— Ow!"

He glared at Ms. Bennett, who had worked hard to accidentally step on his foot with her high heel. "Sorry," she murmured, and settled herself down between him and Mom, even though that was a bit crowded and left me sitting across from all three of them. "Now, Grace," she said before Mr. Kroll or Mom could continue arguing the finer points of transportation in the twenty-first century, "tell me about your sister."

My mind, of course, went blank. What did she want to know? I thought of the time I'd been at my friend Cassandra's house, and Cassandra had been crying, and I asked her what was the matter. "I hate my sister," she said. "I wish she'd never been born."

"What did she do?" I asked.

"She's just mean," Cassandra told me. "*You* know. You have an older sister."

But I hadn't known. Emily had never been mean—or at least not I-wish-she'd-never-been-born mean. When I thought of Emily, I thought of the time she helped me get out of my muddy clothes after Mom said "Don't get your clothes muddy"—and Emily had them in the washing machine, then in the dryer, then hanging back up in the closet before Mom got home.

So I looked at the Rasmussem people, who wanted to know about Emily, and I asked Ms. Bennett, "What about her?"

"Does she have friends?"

"Sure."

Ms. Bennett continued to look at me expectantly. Was I supposed to give names and addresses?

Mom filled in. "Emily has lots of friends. When she was living at home, she would have had a sleepover or gone to somebody else's house every weekend if we'd let her. She loves staying in the dorm—she says it's like a sleepover every day of the week."

"So she's enjoying the college experience?" Ms. Bennett asked.

"Yes," Mom told her, somewhere between proud and snappy, as though she suspected Ms. Bennett was somehow or other criticizing Emily.

"Problems at home?"

Even though Ms. Bennett was still looking at me, and I was shaking my head no, it was Mom who answered. "My husband and I have very good relationships with both our daughters. Don't you go implying that this is somehow our fault."

Mr. Kroll said, "Neither Rasmussem Corporation nor its employees mean to imply—"

Ms. Bennett talked right over him, "And yet Emily's

note clearly shows that she has chosen not to return to her home or college."

Ah, yes, the note. That short, scary note: "Not anybody's fault. This is MY choice." What in the world could that mean? Other than, of course, what it sounded like it meant?

"Well, that's nonsense," Mom was telling Ms. Bennett. "Emily has come home just about every weekend."

Ms. Bennett raised her eyebrows.

Mom supplied the explanation no one had asked for: "Because she still has ties to her high school friends."

She didn't say what she could have: Emily has always been the popular sister. Mom's good about not labeling, for which I can only be thankful, because Emily is the popular one, the smart one, the pretty one—which either leaves me with negatives or with nothing. Dad calls me levelheaded. That's pretty much a last-ditch-effort-to-say-*something* kind of compliment, if you ask me: Grace, her personality is such an inoffensive shade of beige.

"All right," Ms. Bennett said smoothly.

All right? I thought. It was like she was conceding a point in a debate. *Were* we debating?

Ms. Bennett asked, "Boyfriend?"

"Yes," Mom told her. "Frank Lupiano, a nice boy who both Mr. Pizzelli and I approve of."

"Did she meet him at college?" Ms. Bennett asked.

"High school," Mom said. "He's gone to Boston now, but they're always calling or messaging each other. They're still very close."

"Hmmm," Ms. Bennett said. "Is there anything you can think of, Grace? Any unhappiness your sister might have shared with you?" She held up a hand to silence my mother, who was about to protest.

Popular, smart, pretty. If Emily hadn't also been the kind one, I could have hated her. Instead, I wanted to *be* her.

"No," I said. "I can't think of anything."

"We'll let that go for now," Ms. Bennett said. "You tell us if anything comes to mind."

"All right," I said. I could have said that Emily was the well-adjusted daughter in our family. Sure, I have friends, but Emily had more friends than she knew what to do with. She was a joiner, and all you had to do was look at her yearbook to see that there was hardly a club she didn't belong to. And most often, she was voted president of the club.

Me, the only thing I've ever joined was Odyssey of the Mind, and that was because my homeroom teacher bullied me into it. But I dropped out because (a) I am not really team oriented, and mostly (b) I was too worried about freezing up during the spontaneous, or improvisational, part. What if I blurted out something stupid and embarrassed myself? Or what if I couldn't think of anything at all and the whole team failed because of me? Emily didn't have worries like that.

And yet, apparently, she had some sort of worries.

And I was supposed to find out what they were. And talk her out of worrying about them.

Which was another worry for me.

Rasmussem Corporation was founded in Rochester, so the facility on Lake Avenue is both gaming arcade and international headquarters. When we got there, I saw a sign in the front window of the arcade:

CLOSED FOR ROUTINE MAINTENANCE
SORRY FOR THE INCONVENIENCE

Mom saw it, too, and sniffed. "Don't want to scare the paying customers away."

Ms. Bennett, who was getting pretty good with forestalling argument by holding up her hand, held her hand up for Mr. Kroll.

The mobot limo drove around to the back, where we could get out without anyone on the street seeing. Once we were on the sidewalk, the car drove off—presumably to park itself somewhere it wouldn't get ticketed, towed, or de-hubcapped. Ms. Bennett swiped her nametag under a scanner to open the service door.

Someone must have been watching for us, because a young woman in a white lab coat was coming down the hallway to greet us.

"Any change?" Ms. Bennett asked her.

The young woman, who looked about Emily's age, shook her head.

Ms. Bennett told us, "Emily is in gaming cubicle eighteen."

"Can I get you anything?" the girl—her name badge identified her as Sybella—asked Mom. "There's a Tim Hortons next door, and their coffees are pretty good."

Mom looked ready to slap her. "You've gone and gotten my daughter stuck in one of your stupid games, and you're thinking an iced cappuccino is going to make me feel better?"

You could see the Sybella girl thinking like, *Yeah, probably caffeine wasn't the best thing to offer YOU.*

Mr. Kroll—cut off yet again by one of Ms. Bennett's *Silence* gestures—announced, "I'll be in my office if anyone needs me." He hesitated, perhaps debating whether to inform Mom that neither Rasmussem nor any of its employees had been the ones to get Emily stuck in the game, or maybe considering whether he wanted to tell Sybella that *he* would like a cup of coffee. In any case, Ms. Bennett was hustling us down the hall, and he stayed behind.

If you go into Rasmussem to play a game with a group, they put you all together in a room big enough to accommodate however many total immersion couches you need, even though once you're hooked up, you're completely unaware of your physical surroundings and you don't need to be near the people you're playing with. You can play a game with people on a different continent . . . if you happen to be the kind of person who knows people on different continents, or if you don't mind playing with people you don't know. The friends-all-together part is just for those few minutes before they hook you up and after the game is finished.

On the other hand, if you're playing a solitary game, they put you in a room that's only about a couple of feet longer and a couple of feet wider than the total immersion couch itself. Even the word *couch* is a bit of a hyperbole, as what we're talking about here comes closer to a doctor's examining table than anything you're likely to find in a living room.

Ms. Bennett opened a door, and there was Emily lying on her couch in her cubicle. I thought, in my levelheaded way, *We won't all be able to fit in there at once.*

Another part of me taunted, *You're trying to avoid thinking about Emily.* It was true. My mind was flitting from one unimportant detail to another: the size of the cubicle; how Emily was wearing jeans and a white lab coat like the coffee enthusiast who had met us at the door; how her body looked small and little-girlish and unprotected, because if I saw her asleep at home, she'd be wrapped up in a blanket or comforter. I even took in that her eyes were closed but—beneath the lids—were darting back and forth, which I knew was because the Rasmussem experience taps into the same part of the brain where dreams come from. But it was still kind of creepy.

Mom, on the other hand, rushed right into that cubicle and cupped Emily's face in her hands. Then she dropped to her knees beside Emily's couch and began to cry—deep, racking sobs.

I could see Ms. Bennett hesitate before deciding to put her arm around Mom's shoulders. "It's okay, Mrs. Pizzelli. She isn't in pain—the exact opposite, in fact. And we will find a way to get her to come back."

That should be me offering comfort to my mother, I thought. But I've never been very good at that sort of thing—too self-conscious, too concerned about being rebuffed, too afraid of saying the wrong thing and making everything worse. Emily, of course, is a naturally warm and sympathetic person and always knows exactly what to say and do when people are happy or sad or scared.

I WOULD have put my arm around Mom, I thought as I stood there in the hallway.

It was just that Ms. Bennett was faster.

Even though she had hesitated.

If our positions had been reversed, Emily would have put her arms around Mom.

Ms. Bennett made Mom sit down on the edge of the couch, by Emily's feet. There were tissues on the shelf beneath the couch, and Ms. Bennett—taking no chances—handed Mom the whole box.

In an accusing voice, Mom managed to say, "You told me you had disconnected her." She reached out her hand as though to pull loose the feed wires that stretched from Emily's temples to the wall panel behind her.

Ms. Bennett blocked her. "We did," she assured Mom, assured both of us, even though I was still standing lumpishly in the hallway. "But when that didn't do any good, we hooked her up again so that we can monitor her responses and see where—in the game world—she is."

Mom took a deep breath, but her voice shuddered nonetheless. "And now you want to do the same to Grace?"

I forced myself to be calm enough to say, "It doesn't hurt, Mom. It's just suction cups." My mind, always ready to come up with a dire alternative, was quick to chime in: *Or at least, it's never hurt before.*

Ms. Bennett touched a button on the wall panel and the side wall slid down into the floor—instant small-group-sized room.

Little-Miss-Tim-Hortons Sybella was there, waiting to set me up.

"It should be me," Mom said. She once more burst into tears, so I went over to the other couch. No kid should see her parent cry.

And no kid, even a beige, nondescript kid whose best quality is her lack of excitability, should leave her sister stranded and in trouble, even if it's that sister's own choice.

"As soon . . ."—Mom had to work hard to make her words intelligible to me—". . . as soon as you get into the game, come straight back out again, so that I know you can."

I could see Sybella press her lips together to keep from saying anything about how that was useless or a waste of time, but Ms. Bennett said, "That will be fine."

Sybella gave me a hairband to get my forehead clear.

As though she had never seen me with my hair pulled back, Mom dissolved into tears again.

"Do you want to go to the restroom?" Ms. Bennett asked her. "Throw some cold water on your face?" Before I even realized this might have been something to panic over, Ms. Bennett assured Mom, "We won't send Grace till you're back."

Mom nodded, and Ms. Bennett led her out of the room.

"Shoes or no shoes?" Sybella asked. "You don't *need* to take them off, but you might be more comfortable without."

I kicked my sneakers off, only hoping—once it was too late—that my toes weren't beginning to come through my socks. I snuck a peek. No obvious signs of wear, but I wouldn't have chosen the Bugs Bunny pair if I had known anybody was going to see them.

"There's a shelf beneath the couch where you can put your shoes and any personal items," she told me. "They'll be perfectly safe there. No one besides me will be coming in here." She blinked, then added, "Well, and your mother and Ms. Bennett." She patted the couch to indicate which direction for me to lie down—like it wasn't obvious by the pillow at the end near the wall with the panel.

"Need to loosen the button of your jeans? Your clothing shouldn't be tight or restrictive. Again, keep in mind that no one else will be seeing you."

"I'm okay," I told her. "I've done this before."

She nodded emphatically. I noticed that she kept glancing at a clipboard. She wasn't checking things off, but she was making sure she went through the routine correctly. Since I'd played before, she could skip some of the hand-holding instructions, but now she'd lost her place.

"New here?" I asked, because she looked so frazzled.

It wasn't fair. *She* should have been calming *me*. It was *my* sister who was . . . Well, I wasn't sure what was going on with Emily. But she was in *some* sort of trouble.

"Yeah," Sybella said as she slathered my temples with some of that cold jellylike stuff that is supposed to help keep the leads on, but not *stuck* on. "The course description said 'game development and facilitation.' I didn't realize I'd be interacting with the public."

After a few seconds of silence as she triple-checked that the wires were positioned correctly, it sank in that she'd said *course* description, not *job* description. "Are you an intern, too? Like my sister?"

"Yup," she said. "I don't know her. They already asked. I mean, it's a big class."

"You're in her *class*?" I echoed. It was hard to believe they could be in the same school and not know each other. Even people from my grade, three years younger, had known Emily. "So you only met once you both started working here?"

"Not so much," Sybella said.

This was March. Emily had been going to school for almost seven months, working at Rasmussem for three. It was amazing that she hadn't arranged a Get-to-Know-One-Another Ice-Cream Social, or a Halloween party, or a Thanksgiving feast, or a Christmas gift exchange in that time, not to mention a Valentine's Day dance.

Mom and Ms. Bennett came back in. Mom looked like she was holding herself together through sheer will. She sat down on Emily's couch, but on the side near me, and she took my hand.

"Ready, Grace?" Ms. Bennett asked. "We're going to set you down in the game that Emily's development team was working on. Because game time moves much more quickly than real time, we can't pinpoint exactly where she is, but you should be in her vicinity."

"So," my mother asked, "how does Grace get out of the game?"

I knew the answer to that, because that's something they always remind you of just before you go under.

"As with all our games," Ms. Bennett told Mom, "there's a safety feature we've built in, because these games are supposed to be fun. If something seriously spooks one of our players, or if—in this case—Grace wants to confer with us because she's learned something she thinks might be helpful, all she has to do is say: 'End game. Bring me back to Rasmussem.'" To me, she said, "Again, bear in mind it won't be instantaneous because of the time differential, but we'll pull you out if you speak those words—or if we sense by your bio readings that something is severely bothering you. Except for this first time, when we'll just pull you back automatically right away, to assure your mother it can be done."

I couldn't think of any more questions to delay things. "Okay," I said.

"Do I need to let go of her hand?" Mom asked, which I thought was a reasonable question, but apparently not, because Sybella snorted, though she tried to mask it with a cough.

Ms. Bennett must have been getting exasperated, because she said, "It's not like we're giving her electric shock treatment or defibrillating her. Grace, close your eyes and count back from one hundred by sevens."

Why was it always sevens? Last time I'd played, I'd told myself I was going to do some memorizing so as not to embarrass myself, but of course I hadn't gotten around to that. I closed my eyes. "One hundred. Ninety-three . . ." Okay, everything after that was complicated, at least for me, at least without pencil and paper. Okay, seven from fourteen would be seven, so—minus one . . . "Eighty-six." Could they tell if I used my fingers? Did everybody else do this faster? Was I the biggest loser to ever lie down on one of these couches?

I opened my eyes to see if they were laughing at me, and I was in Emily's game.

CHAPTER 3

Emily's Game

NOBODY HAD SAID anything about what kind of game Emily had been working on, but immediately I could see that it was a kids' game. Specifically—and I say that even though normally speaking I hate stereotyping—it was a little girls' game. The colors gave it away: pink and lavender and lilac and violet and teal. Any self-respecting boy would be gagging already. I myself was concerned about instant-onset diabetes from all the sweetness.

It wasn't that I'd been expecting something in particular. But now, forced to think about it, I was amazed to find that Emily was trying to lose herself in a game aimed at ten-year-olds. I guess I'd subconsciously been assuming she'd be in a fantasy medieval world where—as a kick-butt type of warrior queen—she'd be in the middle of high adventure in some exotic locale, menaced by fierce-but-surprisingly-attractive bad guys, and surrounded by her own handsome-and-ready-to-die-for-her company of fighters.

Oh, wait. That was what I would have chosen.

Still, this game looked like PBS programming for kids barely old enough to spell PBS.

I found myself in a white latticework gazebo, sitting on one of those suspended-from-the-rafters porch swings, which was garlanded with fragrant flowers of the afore-mentioned girly-girl colors. To the left of the gazebo was a Victorian-style house—ditto on those colors—sitting on the edge of a little lake, complete with swans. At least the swans were white and didn't look too much like plush toys. To the right was a wooded area—not scary let's-lose-Hansel-and-Gretel-type woods, but almost like a slightly disorderly or-chard with a variety of trees, many of them in full blossom. The trees were obviously more than a background, because there was a path of crushed sparkly white stones leading into them.

A butterfly—an oversized monarch that looked as though it had been tapped by a glitter stick—landed on my hand on the swing's armrest.

"You don't happen to know where Emily is, do you?" I asked the butterfly.

But the thing seemed more interested in being seen than in communicating.

In the games I've played, there's a mechanism gamers call the "Finding Rasmussem Factor." I have no idea what the official name for it is, but it works like this: if all else fails, we're told in a not-so-subtle bit of self-aggrandizing self-promotion to go to Rasmussem. Sometimes that's a person, or it can be an artifact, or a place—someone to meet or something to get or somewhere to go to have the quest explained or to learn the more essential ins and outs of the particular game world you're playing. For most kids, it's a matter of pride *not* to seek Rasmussem, but in some games you absolutely cannot proceed without checking in.

In this case, however, I didn't need to find the purpose of the game; I only needed to find Emily.

I got off the swing. As far as I knew, the Rasmussem people hadn't programmed any changes to my personal appearance, but I saw they'd made my clothing fit in with this world. I was wearing a white floaty dress and delicate silver ballet flats. Something moved near my face in my peripheral vision, and instinctively I put my hand up. Ribbons. Cascading down from a flower crown. Of course.

Standing in the entryway of the gazebo, I looked around.

House.

Lake.

Flower garden.

Woods.

No Emily.

No hint where Emily might be.

Well, I thought, *let's not dismiss the obvious.* "Emily!" I called.

But of course it couldn't be that easy.

I knew Ms. Bennett and Sybella would be pulling me back shortly, but that didn't mean I should just hang around here. That was a waste of time. The recall program could find me wherever I went, and I was worried about Emily. Ms. Bennett had been vague about what would happen if Emily stayed in the game too long. But international companies don't send chief technical engineers and lawyers on trivial errands.

House, I decided. That was a limited space for me to explore.

I stepped out of the gazebo onto the lawn. The grass was as lush and soft as green velvet, and every step released a just-mown scent.

The house had a wraparound porch that completely encircled the place, but there were steps on this side leading to what I presumed to be the front door, complete with iridescent leaded glass.

No doorbell, I noticed.

No lock, either. When I turned the knob, the door opened, and I found myself in a huge foyer with slate tiles in the pastel-heathers family of color. "Emily!" I called.

The place was too kid-friendly to have anything even remotely spooky like an echo. Despite the fact that there was no answer, I could smell sugar and cinnamon, as though someone was baking.

A magnificent stairway curved gracefully to the upstairs rooms. As inviting as that looked, with the red carpet and the shiny wooden banisters, I decided to check the ground floor first.

The rooms were lavishly furnished: grandfather clock in the foyer; orchids and sunflowers and rhododendrons and a pink baby grand piano in the sunroom; cupboards and buffets and a big-enough-for-state-dinners-at-the-White-House table in the dining room; floor-to-ceiling shelves in the library, accessed by a ladder that slid around on a track so that you could reach even the farthest volume on the highest shelf and then read it in one of the big comfy chairs. But no clutter or knickknacks. Nothing personal. No sign that anyone actually lived here.

Nobody in the bright and shiny kitchen, either, despite the crystal bowl with fresh-cut flowers on the counter, and a platter of those aromatic cinnamon cookies. I took one— out of curiosity, not real hunger—and it was warm and delicious. Well, that was *one* thing I liked in this game.

I had just decided I would have to go upstairs after all, when I happened to look out the kitchen window. Which wasn't hard to do. This place had more glass overlooking pretty expanses than a window manufacturer's ad. The particular view I had was of the lake. I could still see the swans, but from this vantage I also noticed a dock—a pretty, flower-festooned dock—which made me look a little farther out onto the water, and that's when I saw another swan shape, a big one. It was, in fact, a swan-shaped boat.

The boat came complete with a man dressed like a Venetian gondolier. Can a boat shaped like a swan *be*, technically speaking, a gondola? Well, I couldn't call this guy a swandolier, even in my head. So, a gondolier was standing in the back of the swan gondola, and he was navigating, leisurely and gracefully moving the boat through the water with a pole that was at least twice as tall as he was.

And there—yes, I'd been looking for her, but I couldn't believe my luck to have actually found her—was Emily. She was wearing a dress every bit as white and gauzy as my own, except she had a straw sun hat instead of a Renaissance Faire flower crown. Reclining in the front part of the boat, she was holding a book with one hand, the other hand lazily dragging in the clear Caribbean-blue-green water.

Relieved to see her safe, I threw open the window— which, unlike every window in *our* house, flew open easily, not sticking for a moment. Very faintly, across the distance, I could hear the gondolier singing about Santa Lucia.

"Emily!" I shouted.

The warm, flower-scented breeze was blowing toward me, which was why I could hear the gondolier, despite the distance, but my voice didn't carry to them.

I tried again, more loudly: "Emily!"

She looked up from her book and cocked her head,

obviously hearing something, but not sure what, or from where.

"EMILY!" I screamed so hard my throat tickled.

Which was when I felt something like a big warm fluffy blanket wrap itself around me.

And then I was back at Rassmussem.

CHAPTER 4

Hello. Remind Me Again Why I'm Here?

COMING OUT of a Rasmussem game is sort of like waking up alert—okay, okay, not that I have much experience with *that*.

But what I'm saying is I wasn't confused, wondering where I was or whether I was dreaming. One moment I was at the window in that designer kitchen, with Emily about to look over and see me, the next I was being wrapped up in a cozy blanket, and then there I was on the total immersion couch looking up into my mother's I-will-be-brave/just-ignore-these-tears-in-my-eyes face.

"Are you okay?" she asked. And right on top of that: "Is your sister okay? Did you see her?"

I had known from the start that this first time, my coming and my going would be one right after the other, that I was—metaphorically speaking—simply testing the water by sticking my toe in. The fact was, I had needed to be reassured just as much as my mother that the Rasmussem equipment wasn't faulty and that I could return to reality at any time; so it was petty to blame my short visit on my mother's technophobia. That I had even found Emily so quickly in the intricacy of the game's many locales was more than anybody could have counted on.

Still, I was frustrated, and for some reason Mom's forced courage grated on my nerves, and it was easier to be mad at her than to admit how helpless this whole situation made me feel.

"I *was*," I snapped, "about to make contact with Emily."

Mom's smile wavered and she blinked rapidly, but her voice didn't give away anything as she said, "How did she seem?"

And that wasn't nearly as easy a question as it should have been.

That note Emily had left, that simple, scary note, sounding—I tried to shy away from the thought but wasn't quick enough—disturbingly like a suicide note . . .

I had expected to see her languishing. Or in a frenzy of not-enough-time-to-think activity.

I glanced beyond my mother to Ms. Bennett and Sybella. "She's in a kids' game. She was on a gondola. Reading a book. Being sung to in Italian."

Mom blinked some more and managed to squeak out, "Well, that sounds nice."

Ms. Bennett said, "It's Land of the Golden Butterflies. We're about to begin beta testing, so it's pretty complete. Emily and several of the others have been playing, intentionally making unusual choices so we could be fairly certain the game wouldn't crash or loop just because some little player decided to feed the unicorn food to the dolphins, or vice versa."

"There's unicorns *and* dolphins?" I asked.

"That's what our focus groups indicate little girls like," Sybella assured me. "And kittens. Not counting media tie-ins, those are the kinds of stuffed animals little girls most often ask for."

I must have rolled my eyes, because Ms. Bennett added, "And for the girls who prefer, there are also dragons and dinosaurs. We're trying to make it a pleasant experience for everyone."

Still . . . I thought.

There's a big difference between what a ten-year-old finds pleasant and what an eighteen-year-old does. Isn't there? I mean, sure, I still have Merry the Christmas Moose on my bed, even though I'm fourteen. And, yeah, despite the fact that I claim she's a seasonal decoration, she never gets put away between January and November. But it's not like I sleep with her. Not usually. My attachment to her is more because of the memories of Grandma and Grandpa, who gave her to me, than because I fantasize about her being alive and able to talk and play.

Ms. Bennett said, "It may have been opportunistic that Emily chose Land of the Golden Butterflies to . . ." She hesitated, because we weren't sure, not one hundred percent sure, what Emily's plan was. We could only surmise. And be anxious about it. Ms. Bennett finished, ". . . to fulfill her purposes. Even though she had access to codes to other games, that was the one her team was working on. So it may well be that she chose it because it would have been the easiest for her to modify."

So what Ms. Bennett was saying was that Emily had decided to lose herself in that particular game because it was there, like that guy—whoever he was—who said he'd climbed Mount Everest because it was there. But just as he'd have found another mountain to go up if Everest *hadn't* been there, it was likely that Emily had made the decision to turn her back on the real world first, and then settled on how.

"All right," I said, antsy to get back, though I had no idea how I was supposed to talk sense into Emily. Surely she knew she couldn't stay hooked up to the equipment indefinitely. That she was risking brain injury, or even death. "Well, no insights, but at least now we know the equipment works. So send me back."

Ms. Bennett looked for confirmation from Mom, who whispered to me, "Be careful," which we all took as a go-ahead.

Sybella said, "Okay, put your head down and close your eyes and count back from one hundred by sevens."

Damn it.

"One hundred," I said.

I pretended I'd misheard. "One hundred seven. One hundred fourteen. One hundred twenty-one. One hundred twenty-eight . . ."

Oops, I was having trouble going in that direction, too.

Uncertainly, I said, "One hundred thirty-two. No, one hundred thirty-five . . ."

But I don't think they heard me, because by then I could hear water slapping against the dock.

Before I even opened my eyes, I thought, *Wow, last time I could see the lake from the gazebo, but I don't think I could hear it.*

Then a voice, a male voice, very close, said, *"Buon giorno. Le piacerebbe fare un giro in gondola?"*

That got my eyes open in a hurry.

Ms. Bennett and Sybella hadn't landed me back in the gazebo; this time I was actually standing on the dock. Too late. Time had continued to pass in the game while I had spent my few minutes back at Rasmussem: Emily was no longer here. The gondolier, looking very handsome in an older-guy Mediterranean sort of way, was standing in his boat, smiling at me. I don't speak Italian, but by the way he had one hand outstretched toward me and the other indicating the seat in the gondola, I guessed he was offering me a ride. I didn't think it was a ride *to* someplace. When I'd seen Emily in the boat earlier, the singing and the leisurely drifting had given me the impression that she hadn't been headed anywhere in particular; just, it had seemed, taking a pleasant outing on the lake. I didn't have time for that.

"No, thank you," I said. In the total immersion games I've played, I've learned it never hurts to be polite, even to virtual characters. I asked, "Where's Emily?"

The man shook his head and said, *"Scusa. Non capisco."*

"I'm looking for Emily," I said, realizing—even as I did it—that I was raising my voice, as though he were hard of hearing, not Italian.

He shrugged and said, *"Non ho capito, ma Le potrei cantare una bella canzone."*

"Emily," I practically shouted at him.

"Emily," he repeated, and kissed his fingertips. But that was all.

I turned to leave him and to head back to the house, hoping that she and I had simply traded places and that I would find her in the kitchen watching me. But the gondolier said, *"Signorina?"*

I turned back, though if he didn't speak English, it wouldn't do me any good even if he *did* know where Emily was, because I wouldn't be able to understand his explanation.

"Delfini," he said.

I shook my head.

He repeated the word and pointed out toward the middle of the lake. A pair of dolphins was leaping in the air.

"Ah," I said. "Lake dolphins." No wonder kids today are confused.

The gondolier was pointing to his boat again, then the dolphins, obviously telling me he could take me closer.

Was he saying . . . ? I mean, this *was* a fantasy game . . . Could Emily have turned herself into . . . ?

I could have kicked myself for not having asked Ms. Bennett and Sybella what the point of this game was. I pointed to the dolphins and asked, "Emily?"

The gondolier looked confused, then gave an expression as though my nose had suddenly broken off and was hanging on to my face by a string of snot. He smacked his forehead with the palm of his hand to indicate he had never heard anything so stupid in his life, and he repeated with exaggerated care, *"DEL-FI-NI."*

Okay. So not Emily.

"Thanks all the same," I said. *"Grazie."* Which I think is Italian. Unless it's Spanish.

Once more his fingers brushed my sleeve. By now he'd seen that talking to me was useless. He pointed to the tall red and white striped pole to which the gondola was tied. Another of those big sparkly butterflies had alighted on top. The gondolier made a gesture of cupping hands and indicated for me to try to catch the butterfly.

Not wanting to miss something important, but still feeling both impatient and like a jerk, I did. For a brief moment, I felt the creature's wings flutter, tickling my palms.

Then it turned cold and solid. Carefully, I unfurled my fingers, and found that the butterfly had turned into a gold coin.

"*Bene,*" the gondolier congratulated me.

I nodded my gratitude for his showing me how things worked here—since my attempt at Italian had apparently all but left him mute. Fortunately, my dress came with pockets, so I put my coin in one. Then I ran down the dock, across the lawn, and into the house through the French doors of the kitchen.

"Emily?" I called.

The house was as quiet and empty as on my first visit.

I searched the ground floor even faster than I had the last time, not letting myself get distracted by wondering what was going on. Once I got back to the kitchen, I *did* check outside the window again, to make sure there wasn't a glitch in the program that made Emily visible on the lake only from that vantage point. The gondolier was alone, standing in his boat, patiently waiting to offer a ride and a song to whoever came by.

Up the grand staircase to the second floor I went. There was a huge huge huge bathroom with two tubs, one an old-fashioned kind with claw feet, the other basically a shallow sunken pool tiled with lapis lazuli. The bedroom had a balcony that overlooked the lake; a dresser with a marble top and a tiltable mirror; and a canopy bed, complete with a small step stool to get up into it. The mood was little-girlish rather than bed-and-breakfast-ish, and when I saw the white furry area rug, I told myself, "Hmph!" Disgruntled by all this frilliness, I permitted myself the unkind thought, *Little girls like unicorns. I wonder if that's unicorn fur.*

I opened a door and found a walk-in closet at least as big as our living room. There were all sorts of princess gowns, Southern-belle gowns, Renaissance gowns. Who could have guessed that Emily, who normally slouched around in jeans and hoodies, had a heart that yearned for dress-up?

But there was no sign of her here, so I ran back downstairs.

I threw open the French doors that took me back out to the porch, and there she was, in the garden.

"Emily!" I called, to keep her from wandering off before I got to her.

She heard me—I caught the quick glance in my direction—but then she looked away.

What?

I'd been frantic to find her, was delighted to succeed, and now she was *ignoring* me?

Like all the fear I'd been feeling, all the turmoil, all the worry about what had happened and the bigger worry about how was I supposed to help—like all that was *nothing?*

I suppose, I told myself with a little bit of self-pity and a good deal of bitterness, *I suppose I should consider myself lucky she's only ignoring me and that she didn't start running away from me even as her name left my lips.*

The possibility that she might not want to see me caused me to slow down, to reevaluate. I saw that she had changed out of the white linen Victorian dress she'd had on in the gondola and replaced it with a tea-length chiffon dress in shades of peach and pink. It kind of made her look like a wood nymph, which was perfect, because she'd put her book away, and now she had a wicker basket over her arm as she collected long-stemmed flowers.

Clearly, this was very important work that required too much concentration to greet her sister, who had come, at some personal inconvenience, to rescue her.

I ran down the porch steps and across the lawn to the flower garden, and stepped directly in front of her. Despite her lack of enthusiasm, I was ready to throw my arms around her and hug her, but she still wouldn't make eye contact.

"Emily!" I repeated, to show her how glad I was to see her. But she was deep into snipping the stem of a blood-red amaryllis with her sparkly scissors.

She looked more annoyed than anything else, her expression similar to the one my mother uses when our neighbors' badly trained puppy barks and jumps on her and rudely sniffs where Mom doesn't want to be sniffed.

Emily stepped around me as though I were a muddy spot on the path and reached for a yellow and orange daffodil. Then a spotted tiger lily. Then a purple and white gladiolus.

I moved in front of her again. Though my heart was breaking, I repeated, in my most please-please-please voice, "Emily!"

She made to sidestep me once again, and I threw my arms around her, basket and scissors and all.

And she finally opened up to me.

"Geez, Grace," she complained, and disentangled herself. She didn't exactly push me away, but she made no attempt to hide how peeved she was that I'd crunched her basket. She picked up the gladiolus and frowned at the stem, which now bent at an angle. She snipped the broken part off, but this made it significantly shorter than the rest. "It probably won't work now," she muttered in a disgusted tone.

"Flowers here *work?*" I asked. Of all the things I *could* have said, this was not what I would have guessed would be my first question for her. But apparently we needed something more to connect than simply my being overjoyed to find her.

Evidently, "Flowers here *work?*" was a stupid question.

She sighed, then glanced at the flowers she'd gathered. This garden was a jumble, with an assortment of blooms. Our grandmother had been a gardener, both in Rochester and at her winter home in Gainesville, Florida, and I recognized that many of the flowers in this garden bloomed under different climate conditions and at different times of year from one another. Emily held up a finger—I guess to forestall my lunging into another hug and crushing some more of her precious flowers—then leaned over to clip a bluish-purple iris. She tossed the iris into the basket.

And the iris disappeared. Along with the other irises that had been in there.

Emily lifted the mass of remaining flowers to show me the gold coins accumulated at the bottom of the basket. "A coin," she explained, "for every ten flowers of the same kind."

"Wow," I said. "That's amazing."

I guess she picked up on the sarcasm.

"What are you doing here, Grace?" she asked.

"What am *I* doing here? I'm here to help you, you idiot. What are *you* doing?"

"I'm gathering flowers," Emily said, walking around me, as though that explained all and I could go home now.

I followed her as she meandered down the path collecting blossoms. I wanted to say, "Mom's worried sick." I wanted to say, "I've been worried sick." But when it became obvious that Emily had finished explaining, I backed off from the Big Questions, such as "You don't want to die, do you?" Instead, I asked, "So what do you do with all those coins?"

"Duh!" A black-eyed Susan apparently completed a set, for it disappeared as Emily added it to her basket. "You were in the house, weren't you?" she asked. "Wasn't that you in the kitchen? Tell me it wasn't that overbearing Ms. Bennett eating my cookies and opening my windows."

"That was me," I confirmed.

Once again, the conversation seemed to have reached a dead end.

"The house . . . ?" I urged her, since that—at least—seemed like something she was willing to talk about.

"It didn't build itself," she said. "It didn't furnish itself."

"Okay," I said. This explained nothing. "Emily," I asked, "what's going on?"

Emily sighed. "Follow me," she said, then added—making no attempt to keep me from hearing—"Yeah, like I could stop you."

There was a wall of bushes—tall, taller than us—and that's where Emily led me. It was only when we'd come to a space formed by two of the bushes that I caught on. "A maze," I said, seeing the path before us. "A topiary maze."

"Yup," Emily agreed. "Just let me get a couple things here, then we can sit down and talk." She turned right, then left, then left again, and there was an urn of lavender chrysanthemums. Emily cut off all seven of the flowers and tossed them into the basket.

"Two more," she said. Either she'd helped design this maze or she'd navigated it quite a few times, for she seemed entirely familiar with its twistings and turnings. We came to another pot, this one holding hollyhocks. I thought I was doing a good job with hiding how impatient I was getting, but maybe not, because she said, "You can save us some time." She pointed the way we'd been walking. "Around that corner"—it was a right-hand turn—"then take the second left, and there's a vase holding a gerbera daisy. If you can get that for me while I pick these, then we can go back and drink some lemonade on the porch and discuss things."

"Okay," I said.

It only worked as far as "take the second left." There was no vase.

And when I retraced my steps to the pot of hollyhocks—which were all still there, by the way—there was no Emily, either.

CHAPTER 5

Amazed

WELL, what kind of idiot was I? One of the first things Ms. Bennett had said to me was that she had followed Emily into the game to try to talk her out, and Emily had refused to listen. Why had I expected her to listen to me?

It wasn't as though Emily had accidentally gotten stuck in here. The note she'd left behind proved *that*. For whatever reason, she had *chosen* this. What had made me think she was just hanging around waiting for me to lead her home? Especially after her cool reaction to seeing me. If I'd been paying proper attention, I'd have taken the hint when Emily asked whether it was me or Ms. Bennett who'd been watching her from the kitchen. Ms. Bennett probably wasn't so easy to fool.

Okay, well, I wouldn't be, either, next time.

I would just backtrack along the path we had taken into this topiary maze, find her again, and not be so readily put off. Right turn. Left. I would just backtrack . . .

Oops, wait a minute, that couldn't be the way. Make

48

that another right. Hmmm . . . Was that the urn the chrysanthemums had been in? I thought so, but there was a rosebush growing in it. Which either meant flowers here could change—entirely possible—or this was a different urn we hadn't passed before. Also possible. Two right turns and a left . . . Or was that a right and two lefts? Neither way led to the pair of tall bushes that had formed the entry.

So . . . forget trying to backtrack. I had to figure my way out without relying on my demonstrably bad memory of how I'd gotten here.

Oh, yeah, and I forgot to mention: I hate mazes. They just strike me as aggressive pointlessness.

At least fifteen frustrating minutes later (not to mention a whole bunch of bushes and urns full of flowering plants), I was seriously considering announcing to the Rasmussem people that I wanted to get out. They could pluck me out of the maze, then drop me off in Emily's vicinity, which they seemed pretty good at. But it would take several minutes for me to revive into reality and then be put back under into the game world, which would be like another hour for Emily. I had to believe that the longer she spent in this world, the harder it would be to get her to leave.

And that eventually (hours and hours from now, I could only hope, and by that I was thinking *real* hours, not these fleeting game hours), the Rasmussem equipment would somehow fail. Ms. Bennett hadn't explained—at least not to me—what exactly that approximately-eight-hour time limit meant. Maybe that the machine/brain interface would somehow burn out Emily's brain. Or put her into an irreversible coma. Or she might starve to death. Okay, probably not that last, I reassured myself. They could always hook up an IV. Truth be told, I hadn't wanted to know—still didn't want to know—the specifics. I was scared enough already. It was sufficient that I knew I had to convince Emily to come home, whatever her reasons for wanting to lose herself here.

While I was thinking about all that—and wondering if the Rasmussem people could read my moods and feelings (severe embarrassment: would I have to explain that I'd lost Emily mere moments after their expensive equipment had found her for me?)—I became aware of a sound. Music? It was kind of like the high notes of a harp. Or a xylophone. Or . . . maybe . . . a music box.

And yet . . . not.

I made a right-hand turn and found myself in a little clearing. So, my keen instincts had led me to the exact center of the maze rather than back out. There was a pretty little park bench complete with its own canopy to provide shade, and, directly centered, a water fountain—not the kind you find in school halls and near public restrooms, but the ornamental kind, with a fat marble goldfish spouting an arc of water up into the air and down into a blue stone bowl.

The musical noise I was hearing came from there, along

with the relaxing splash of water. I took a step closer, hoping the water would look clean enough to drink, because I was hot and thirsty, as well as cranky. I suspected this world was too nice to have poison or even bacteria-infested water. But I was really hoping the only fish was the marble one. It would be hard to bring myself to drink water—even virtual water—from a bowl that had fish swimming in it—even virtual fish. My brain could tell me one thing, but my gag reflex was already making its point of view clear.

No fish.

Sigh of relief.

"Hello. Welcome," a tiny voice called out.

"Hello, hello," came another voice, and I knew it was another, despite the fact that it sounded just like the first, because the greetings overlapped a bit.

I became aware of two little creatures sitting on the tail of the marble fish. They were about as tall as pencils, and beautiful. Pixies, fairies, elves—something like that. They looked human—if you didn't hold their iridescent wings and hair the color of sherbet against them.

While my own hair was sticking to my sweaty face, occasionally stinging my eyes or getting caught in my teeth, the pixie girls' hair (one green like lime, the other a soft raspberry-purple) billowed prettily in the breeze. They also had gorgeous dresses that appeared to be made of flower petals. Sure, my dress had been okay to start with, but it had gone from being cute to being a nuisance—too much fabric for a warm day, and the grass stains would never come out of the hem. I had taken off the flower-and-ribbon crown the third or fourth time it tipped down over my eyes, and I'd left it around an urn I suspected I'd passed several times already.

"Hello," I answered the pixie girls.

They giggled. Mystery solved. That had been the almost-music sound I'd heard earlier.

"Wishes for coins," one—or maybe it was both—of them told me.

I remembered the butterfly coin I'd caught by the gondola. I took the coin out of my pocket. "What kind of wishes?" I asked.

"Any kind," the raspberry-sherbet-haired pixie giggled.

Lime giggled, too. "Whatever you want. The more coins, the more you can wish for."

"I only need one. Can you send me to wherever Emily is?" I congratulated myself on being clever enough to ask beforehand, and not waste a wish on something they couldn't grant.

"Yes," they both agreed, indicating by their laughter that nothing could be easier, nothing could make them happier.

Though other things here had annoyed me in their excessive girlyness, these two were just so sweet, it was hard not to giggle right along with them. But I wasn't here to be charmed by how cute things were. "How does this work?" I asked.

"Coins go in the fountain . . ." Lime told me in her gleeful little voice.

". . . and wishes get granted," Raspberry finished. Giggle, giggle.

Together they said: "That's what we're here for: to grant wishes."

The quest games I was used to playing weren't this straightforward. I tossed the coin into the fountain. "I wish to be sent where Emily is."

The musical quality of their laughter filled the clearing. Sparkles danced before my eyes. My skin tingled. The topiary maze faded around me.

Then the sparkles dissolved, and I found myself on the very edge of a large chasm. The ground beneath my feet shifted, crumbling. I looked for something to grab hold of, but there wasn't anything.

There wouldn't have been time, anyway.

The ground, a thin lip of earth overhanging that deep, deep expanse, gave under my weight. I bumped. I bounced. I slid. I scraped. Down the face of the cliff, faster and faster I fell. Only after losing half the skin on my hands and knees did I manage to catch hold of a scraggly bush.

Damn pixies.

My arms were already beginning to shake with the

strain of supporting me as I dangled in the air. I had to look down to try to find a solid place to put my feet.

There was a whole lot of down.

Heights are another of those things I hate.

Just look straight ahead, I told myself. Straight ahead was rock and dirt and one itty-bitty bush.

One of my little silver ballet flats had been scraped off my foot without my even noticing. *Still*, I told myself, *that actually might work out for the best*. I tried to dig my toes into the ungiving surface.

I had yet to find a toehold when the bush that anchored me gave up on the whole hopeless situation and came out of the ground. I caught a dizzying flash of sky—which told me that I was tumbling through the air.

That couldn't be good.

Then I felt a fizzy sensation, like when you're drinking ginger ale and it goes up your nose—except this was all over. I'd had that sensation when I'd played other Rasmussem games—the kind *not* meant for little kids—when I'd received grave injuries in a swordfight or some other misadventure. It was the Rasmussem equivalent of dying, and it meant the game was over.

CHƎPƮƎR 6

Adam's Report

T HIS TIME I definitely woke up confused. My mother was shouting—and under normal circumstances, my mother is not a shouter—but she was obviously furious. "What the *hell* were you thinking? How could you be so stupidly thoughtless?"

Sure, I'd been foolish, first walking out of eyesight of Emily, then trusting those treacherous pixies, then . . . what? Not holding on to that sad excuse of a bush tightly enough? Faulting my lack of upper-body strength didn't exactly seem fair. Still, I managed to squeak out, even before opening my eyes, "Sorry. I'll do better next time, really."

And then I did open my eyes just in time to see Mom swing around to face me. Her color went from bright, angry pink to what-have-I-done gray. "Oh, sweetie," she said, her eyes filling with tears as she rushed to take my hand. "No, no, I wasn't talking to you. My poor brave, sweet sweetie." She was patting my face, being careful of the lead wires that were still connected.

Someone else was also saying she was sorry, and for a moment I thought it was Emily. Had Emily come back, too? Because as far as I was concerned, she *did* have a lot to apologize for.

But then I realized the speaker was Sybella.

She continued, "I never thought . . . I mean, a gamer would know . . ."

Ms. Bennett interrupted: "Sybella, why don't you get Adam to come in here, please?"

Without argument, Sybella left. She looked relieved to be going.

To my mother, Ms. Bennett said, "I am so sorry, Mrs. Pizzelli. That was such an unfortunate thing for her to say, but in the context of games, she never stopped to think—"

"What happened?" I asked. "Has something gone wrong with Emily?" Duh. Of course I meant: *Has something gone MORE wrong with Emily than that she won't come out of what has to be the world's most boring and irritatingly insipid total immersion game—sort of Barney Visits Candy Land and Goes to Visit Mr. Rogers' Neighborhood?*

Mom said, "That stupid girl—"

"It was an honest mistake." Ms. Bennett turned to me and explained, "Your signal went flat, and your mother asked what happened, and Sybella said that you'd died." To Mom, Ms. Bennett added, very emphatically, "There is no way Grace can be in physical danger here, Mrs. Pizzelli. We told you that already. Yes, Sybella didn't think before speaking, but that's because she didn't take into account your lack of familiarity with gaming. Characters die—and recover—all the time in the context of games. Far from wanting to upset you, Sybella was trying to put your mind at ease."

Mom had been too badly scared to be willing to forgive so quickly. "Still—"

"Still," Ms. Bennett said, "she's gone. Adam will help us out from now on."

Mom is basically a nice person, so—mad as she was—she couldn't help asking, "You're not saying you're firing her, are you?"

Ms. Bennett, basically a clever businesswoman—one who knew she was facing the real chance of lawsuit regardless of what Mr. Lawyer Kroll might want everyone to believe—countered with, "Do you want her fired?"

Mom considered, then said, "No. I just don't want her in here with us anymore."

Ms. Bennett nodded. "Done." She returned her attention to me. "So what happened?"

"Murderous pixies," I explained.

With a quick glance at Mom, Ms. Bennett assured both of us, "There are no murderous pixies in Land of the Golden Butterflies."

"Yeah, well, tell that to the ghoulish pair of whatever-they-weres that dangled me over a cliff."

"Do you mean mountain gnomes?" Ms. Bennett asked. "Are you saying they actually held you up over a cliff and then let you drop?"

Gnomes made me think of those little statues people have in their gardens: solid, chunky bearded guys.

"No, these were more like Barbie dolls," I said, "but with hair the color of jelly beans." In what I have to say was a pretty good imitation of their oh-so-cute wee little voices, I said, "Ooo, let us help you: wishes for coins." Admittedly losing some of the quality of my impersonation, I finished with a certain amount of bitterness, "Never mind that we'll take your money, then drop-kick you from a great height."

"Sprites," Ms. Bennett said.

Sprites . . . pixies . . . whatever. I thought she was being intentionally contrary in refusing to respond unless I got the words exactly right.

She asked, "What do you mean, they drop-kicked you from a great height? They actually pushed you?"

"Well, not so much *pushed*," I had to admit. What was this sudden need for precision? Had she been taking lawyering lessons from Mr. Kroll? "But they told me I could have a wish, and I asked if they could send me to where Emily was, and they said yes, and instead, they sent me over a very tall, steep cliff."

A male voice from the doorway asked, "How many coins did you give them?"

I looked up to see a guy at least a few years older than

Emily but not yet *old*, maybe twenty-one or twenty-two. He kind of reminded me of Emily's boyfriend, Frank Lupiano, except with better hair. And broader shoulders. And, generally speaking, a more intelligent expression. Actually, he looked a lot better than Frank.

Because I am so quick on my feet and such a great conversationalist, I said, "Huh?"

"Did you give them two coins?" he asked. "Three?"

"Just the one."

I saw him glance at Ms. Bennett.

"What?" I demanded.

Good-Looking—he had to be the Adam Ms. Bennett was substituting for Sybella—said, "Wishes start at one coin, but they get more expensive depending on how complicated they are."

"So they took my money and tried to kill me for short-changing them?" I asked.

Adam shook his head. "They didn't try to kill you." Before I could protest, "You weren't there," he said, "They only granted you a portion of your wish. The kind of spell you asked for, transporting you . . . well, I don't know without looking it up how much it would cost, but more than one coin. You gave them a portion of what the wish cost, so the sprites transported you a portion of the way there. Like getting tossed out of a taxi when your fare exceeds what you've paid for. It was just coincidence that your money ran out while you were passing over the edge of a cliff."

"So you're saying it was my own fault?" If I'd been more daring, I could have pointed out that Rasmussem seemed to be saying that everything that went wrong was my family's own fault.

"Well, yes," Adam said. Then he gave a smile nice enough to make me feel inclined to forgive him his lawyerly ways. "But it shouldn't have happened. I've made a note." He handed Ms. Bennett the clipboard he had carried into the room. To her, he said, "No callbacks from the boyfriend yet, or the roommate, but I spoke to the Residence Advisor at her dorm, and one of the teachers. I asked Sybella to cover Emily's phone contact list."

Ms. Bennett read over what he'd handed her and said, "Hmmm."

Mom put things together faster than I did. "You're checking up on the people who know Emily?"

"Yes," Ms. Bennett said.

"I already told you she's doing well in school and she has lots of friends."

"So you did."

Mom shook her head, obviously miffed.

But I could see Ms. Bennett's point. It's like when you've lost something, and you search in all the places it should be, and it's not there. You have to start checking in places it shouldn't be, because if it were where it was supposed to be, it wouldn't be lost. Obviously, we had missed something about Emily.

Since this guy Adam was somewhat reminiscent of Emily's Frank, I figured she had to have hit it off with him, even if—for whatever reason—she had neglected to befriend coworker Sybella. So I asked him, "Do you know my sister?"

"I'm engaged," he said.

Which was a lot more, and a lot less, than I had asked.

"Congratulations," I told him.

"I met her." He squirmed. "We never really talked."

I glanced at Ms. Bennett to see if she looked as skeptical as I felt sure I looked. But her face didn't give anything away, and she didn't say anything.

Mom didn't seem to have caught that exchange—probably because she wasn't interested in Adam, only Emily. She asked, "So what does Emily's RA say about her?"

"That she's quiet," Ms. Bennett said. "A bit of a loner."

Mom snorted—which I would have done, too, except what if I snorted and something came out? I was trying to appear cool for Adam—even if he *was* seven or eight years too old for me, and walking around announcing his prenuptial status. Mom said, "Then this RA doesn't know her well. Or has her confused with someone else."

Ms. Bennett said, "And the teacher, her psych professor, says she's got a good solid C."

That didn't sound like Emily, either. Her marks were generally better than mine. And she had been telling our parents all semester long that she was doing fine.

"This is all wrong," Mom said.

Well, no kidding.

Mom turned to me. "Did you see Emily? Did you learn anything?"

Facing her please-please-please-give-me-something expression, I couldn't tell her how Emily had been so . . . so . . . Is *underwhelmed* a word? So the-opposite-of-excited to see me. And how she had intentionally ditched me, first chance she got. "Nothing useful," I told her.

Ms. Bennett raised her eyebrows but didn't ask for details.

Before Mom could put me on the spot, Adam asked, "Ready to go under again?"

"I guess."

He must have picked up on some subtle clues that my enthusiasm was less than cheerleaderish. "You're doing fine," he assured me. "Any game takes a bit of getting used to. You're a good kid. And Emily's a good kid, too. You'll connect."

Maybe this wouldn't have sounded like such a bland, empty platitude if he hadn't just finished saying he hardly knew her, and if he hadn't met me only about seven seconds earlier.

Oh, yeah, seven . . .

"Seven," I said before he could ask me. "One hundred and seven, two hundred and seven, three . . ."

CHAPTER 7

Some Enchanted Evening

I WAS BACK in the gazebo, which I guess was better than being halfway through a fall off a cliff or being back in the maze. But my lack of progress was making me cranky. I almost swatted at the glittery butterfly that alighted on the swing next to me, but then I thought better of it. Sure, one gold coin was just about useless, but if the game's designers were providing so many opportunities to get coins, money must be important. I caught the butterfly and put the resulting gold coin in my pocket.

I'd figured we'd go to total restart, but I guess Ms. Bennett and Adam didn't want me to lose what few experience points I might have accidentally managed to accumulate. Either that or they couldn't restart since I'd interacted— Ha! If you want to call it that!—with Emily. So there I was with the same old clothing I'd been wearing right up to my plummet off the edge of the cliff, the dress sweaty and grass-stained, one silver ballet slipper missing in action. A change out of my Victorian dress with its long skirt and full-length sleeves and waist-nipping torso would make me feel much more comfortable. Not that I'd ever go Emily's route and gold-coin-wish myself into a closetful of frills. Still, for a moment I wondered how much the sprites would charge for a nice-fitting pair of jeans. But I knew dealing with those guys was just asking for trouble.

And what kind of girl frets about her clothing while her sister is in desperate need of rescuing? There were so many levels on which I could be anxious about Emily, starting with worrying about what had happened to get her to write that note, and ending with the almost paralyzing dread of what the result would be if I couldn't talk her into coming back with me. Once the panic from *that* thought subsided a bit, I stopped mentally grousing about my dress, which was when I noticed that things had changed. The sky over the lake was dramatically pink and orange and iridescent: sunset. Pretty, but I could only wonder what night would bring in Emily's world.

Another big difference was that the house was now sparkling with lights. There were candles in every window, and the pillars and railing of the porch were strung with little white Christmas bulbs. Very festive.

There was also music playing—the kind you hear in movies set in the time of kings and queens; as in: the king and queen request the honor of your presence at the royal ball. Not the kind of thing I'd ever have suspected Emily would put on her playlist.

I walked into the house, following the music and the chatter of conversation into what had formerly been the dining room. The furniture was gone. All four walls were lined with mirrors that caught and reflected the candlelit crystal chandelier hanging from the ceiling. Turned out the music was being played by four men—wearing powdered wigs, no less—a violinist, a cellist, a harpsichordist, and an I-have-no-idea-what-ist, who had an instrument that might have been second cousin twice removed to a guitar. Meanwhile, a roomful of men and women in elegant garb chattered and laughed while they waltzed or did a reel or minuet or some sort of dance. It was like I'd walked into one of Marie Antoinette's parties—before she lost her head, of course.

While I was still taking all this in, a young man came up to me. By the gold braid and shiny brass buttons on his coat, I could only assume he must be an officer in the military. And while I was distracted by thinking, *Wow, no wonder people talk about the attractions of a guy in uniform*, he bowed and held his hand out to me.

Well, that was all very nice, but, "Sorry," I said, "I'm only here looking for Emily."

The women in the room had these tall, elaborate—but kind of pretty if you overlooked their goofiness—white wigs, and they had dresses that accentuated bosoms while minimizing waists; plus there were necklaces and bracelets and tiaras of diamond, ruby, sapphire, emerald, and probably a lot more gems than I had names for. All of which gave them a kind of sparkly, lovely, grown-up likeness to each other, so I couldn't even tell if Emily was in that crowd. All those mirrors reflecting everything—and reflecting each other reflecting everything—added to the disorienting confusion.

And then, on top of everything else, I felt that soul-draining realization that a girl gets when she notices she's drastically underdressed.

Which was stupid under the circumstances.

But I still noticed.

Of course, in this crowd I would have been outclassed even if my dress had been clean and I'd had two shoes.

I was annoyed with myself for being self-conscious.

The young captain—lieutenant? admiral?—had not backed off, even though I'd ignored him. He still wore that shy but hopeful smile as he continued to hold his hand out to me, an offer, I could tell, to dance.

It was difficult not to feel flattered, even if this *was* only a silly game.

Still, I told this gallant young man, "Really. No."

I stepped into the bewigged, bejeweled wall of dancers—and came close to colliding with a couple who only had eyes for each other.

My guy—okay, okay, I was already thinking of him that way—was right behind me, and he whisked me out of danger. But he didn't do that by pulling me back: he did it by angling me into the swirling mass of elegant dancers.

His left hand held mine; his right was gently but firmly on my back.

"I don't dance," I told him.

He didn't need that warning: I'd already stepped on his feet twice and my own once.

His smile never wavered. Brave man.

I could blame my lack of dancing skill on my being off balance with one bare foot, or on my fear of getting those bare toes stepped on by someone wearing big boots or high heels, but really, I am just a bad dancer.

Well, I thought, *this is one way to check out the room.*

Craning my neck to scan the faces near and far for Emily's did nothing to improve my technique, but my partner was so fluid that he kept us from running down any innocent bystanders, and he never winced when my feet mistook his feet for the floor.

Despite my best intentions, despite—or maybe because of—my mind-numbing worry for Emily, despite my despising this silly, sappy game that worked under the assumption that little girls were all silly and sappy, it was kind of nice to be dancing with a cute guy, even a virtual cute guy. I was feeling . . . well, not graceful, but not clumsy as a three-legged hippopotamus, either. I realized I had sort of a death grip on my partner's hand, and I said, "Sorry"—I was saying that a lot, I noted—and loosened my fingers. My hands were sweaty, but he had white gloves on, so hopefully he couldn't feel that.

Hello, I told myself. *He's a computer simulation. Concentrate.*

There! For a second, I thought I'd found Emily, but it was only a trick of the mirrors, my own reflection glimpsed over my escort's shoulder as we turned around and around and around the room. *Whoa!* I thought, because never before had I realized that as I'd gotten older, I'd come to resemble Emily, at least a little bit. There was hope for me yet.

"Sorry," I said once more as this thought caused me to nearly trip and my ever-vigilant partner held me upright. "I'm looking for Emily. Have you seen her?"

He didn't answer. He only looked at me with eyes that said his devotion to me was unlimited and unfailing. Which, believe me, does have its own charm.

"Emily?" I repeated.

My mind flitted back to the gondolier, who spoke no English. But he had known Emily's name. *"Delfini?"* I said, picking out the one Italian word I remembered.

This guy's smile stayed the same, and he never missed a beat of the dance.

Maybe Emily had populated her world with an international assortment of peoples. *"Hola,"* I said, though I'd just barely squeaked through Spanish in seventh grade.

"¿Dónde está el baño?" That was the first phrase Señora Ra-
mierez had taught us, as finding out where the closest bathroom is can be vital to one's survival, in a foreign land or
not. What else did I remember? *"Hasta la vista?"* Okay, not
Spanish. *"Sprechen Sie Deutsch? Moo goo gai pan? Shalom?
Kumbaya? Waltzing Matilda?"* That about exhausted my
knowledge of foreign phrases. I switched back to English.
"Okay, let go."

He wouldn't.

At least the gondolier had spoken Italian; this guy
didn't seem to speak at all.

Just as that thought nibbled at the edge of my brain,
there was a moment of relative quiet.

Harpsichord, violin, cello, and whatever the heck that
other guy was playing paused as the musicians finished one
piece and turned their sheet music to the next page. I could
hear the rustle of the many-petticoated dresses, the clink of
wineglasses, the soft murmur of conversation.

Of female conversation.

My back had been all sweaty, but now my dress clung
cold and wet to my skin.

Only the women were talking. None of the men. *Not.
A. One.* They just held their partners, looked good, and
smiled.

I yanked my hand out of my dance partner's gloved
grip and twisted away from the arm that encircled me.
"Stop," I commanded him.

He bowed. He backed away. Still smiling.

Creepy.

The music resumed. Alone, I stood in a sea of dancing couples who gracefully twirled their way around me. I was aware of my vulnerable bare foot, but they all knew what they were doing: no one stepped on me.

Another young man approached, offering his hand for this new dance, and I swatted his arm. Yes, I had to be heard over the music, but my voice was louder than it needed to be as I told him, "Leave."

He did.

These guys might have been disturbing in their oddness, but the good thing was that they weren't threatening.

At least, not yet.

I made my way to a wall, where yet another young man—this one a servant, I was guessing—offered me a cup of punch.

Enough was enough. I upended the cup over his head.

He bowed, as though that were his whole purpose: Chief Servant in Charge of Having Drinks Dumped on Him.

With my back to the mirrored wall, and warning off any would-be dance partners or snack offerers with a snarl, I finally caught sight of Emily.

I elbowed my way to where she was dancing with a young man who looked pretty much like all the others: handsome and hollow. None of the dancers seemed to mind my crashing through them, doing my personal interpretation of a rampaging moose.

At this point in this particular dance, each man was holding his partner's hand in the air while the woman walked around him as though he were a Maypole.

"*There* you are," Emily said to me as she continued to circumnavigate her partner. "Did you lose yourself in the maze?"

It was disconcerting to try to keep up a conversation with someone on the move—especially as I must have been the only one who didn't understand the rules of this stupid dance. Partners linked arms with new partners and twirled away in unexpected directions. But follow I did. I bit back my answer—that *she* was the one who'd lost *me*. Could I be mistaken? Had I simply taken a wrong turn?

But I shook off my doubt. She hadn't called for me when I hadn't returned. She hadn't answered when I'd called for her. The maze couldn't be so big that she'd been unable to hear me—definitely not in the few moments we'd been separated before I'd started looking for her.

"You ditched me," I said.

I wasn't sure she heard me over the music. Emily completed a complicated turn with her dance partner before saying, not very forcefully, "Nonsense."

Nonsense? She couldn't even summon up enough emotion or energy for more than a bored *Nonsense?*

This wasn't the Emily I knew. That Emily had refrained from snitching to our parents when she'd been walking down the hall of our elementary school and had seen Mrs. Cooper chewing me out for talking in line. That Emily had taught me how to bake chocolate chip cookies so that I would never go hungry. That Emily had sat up with me the night Grandma died, when Mom was overcome with her own sorrow and Dad was busy contacting all the cousins. That Emily would have told me "No way!" Or "Damn right, and I'll do it again!"

But not "Nonsense."

At this point she and her partner were in a ring with four other couples, each pair of dancers twirling around, while the ring also went around and around. I felt like a little kid watching a carousel and trying to keep track of her favorite horse. "Emily, we need to talk."

"Later," she told me. "After the cotillion."

"Yeah," I said, "lemonade on the porch."

Smiling dreamily into the face of her young man, she said, "You never showed up."

Oops, another partner exchange. I had to scramble to keep up, and was talking to her back. She couldn't make me doubt myself again. "Neither did you. Otherwise when those homicidal sprites moved me halfway to you, I would have ended up in the garden that's between the maze and the porch." In the mood I was in, I wouldn't have put it past her to have intentionally positioned herself somewhere that had the chasm as its halfway point.

Sounding more amused than concerned, she asked, "Homicidal? Did those darling little sprites give you a hard time?"

That was it. My patience snapped. I wanted to shake some sense into her, some sibling loyalty. I settled for grabbing her arm to get her to stop dancing.

The guy she was with took hold of my wrist and squeezed until it hurt, until I let go of my sister—all the while still smiling his bland smile.

Never raising her voice—as though I was only somewhat annoying, like a mosquito's whine—Emily told him, "She's not welcome here."

Not welcome? It was one thing to see it, another to hear it.

I tried, unsuccessfully, to wrench myself free. "Emily?" I said as he pulled on my arm, dragging me away from her and toward the door.

"Emily!" I called, but she just kept on twirling in that circle of dancers.

I caught hold of the door frame to slow down my unceremonious removal from the room.

"Stop!" I said emphatically, remembering how *my* dance partner had responded to a direct command. "Let go!"

Apparently, Emily's commands superseded mine.

Emily's former partner pried my fingers loose from the door frame, then he hoisted me onto his shoulder, fireman-style—rump-side up, as though this wasn't undignified enough.

"Emily!" I yelled, twisting around only to see my sister dancing with a new partner.

She'd betrayed me. She'd betrayed me and didn't even have a guilty conscience about it.

I was carried down the hall, across the festively lit porch, and down the stairs to the lawn—where I was dumped on the grass. And then Emily's strong-and-silent-type guy turned and went back inside, slamming the door behind him.

Emily couldn't just reject me like that.

I was really mad now, so I picked myself up, climbed the porch stairs, and went to open the door.

One more thing new since the last time I'd been here: the door was locked.

CHAPTER 8

Locked Out

I YELLED, "Emily, you're a jerk!" I pounded the door. When that got no reaction, I kicked it. Of course, that would have been a mistake even if I'd done it with my ballet-slippered foot. But with my bare toes, it was a *big* mistake. "Emily, I hate you!" I shouted.

I regretted the words even as they were coming out of my mouth. I didn't hate her. I *greatly disliked* her at this point in our lives, but "hate" was what I felt for this pink, fluffy, infuriatingly mindless game, not my sister.

Still, what was the matter with her? What could be so wrong with her life that she would choose to lose herself in a beautiful but shallow world surrounded by beautiful but shallow guys? Didn't she realize what her rejecting me— rejecting me in favor of this sugary garbage—was putting me through?

It wasn't that there was any chance she could hear me—not with that quartet playing so loudly—but I couldn't leave my "I hate you" hanging in the air.

But I wouldn't apologize for it, either.

Instead, I amended my earlier comment. "Emily," I grumbled, "you're a selfish jerk!"

That made my heart feel better, if not my toes.

The wraparound porch put the windows—at least the ones on the ground floor—within easy reach, so I stomped my way to where I could see into the . . . well, whatever it had been before, it was a ballroom now. The window wouldn't slide up or swing open, at least not from outside, so I rapped my knuckles against the glass.

That must not have been loud enough to counteract Mozart or Strauss or Sousa or whatever that music was.

I fished the butterfly coin out of my pocket and used that to tap-tap-tap on the window, figuring maybe the sharp sound would cut through the festive hubbub of Emily's party. And yes, inside, a few of the guests on the fringe of the crowd turned to look at me. I put my face up to the glass and yelled, "Emily! *Emily!*"

Maybe they couldn't make out my words, but surely someone would understand and fetch her.

Instead, they fetched a servant, who came over and— without so much as making eye contact—pulled the velvet drapes closed, shutting me and the other nighttime nuisances out.

Maybe it was even Emily who'd given the order. I was beginning to wonder if *anything* in this game happened without her say-so.

I mentally told her, *You can't get rid of me THAT easily*.

The evening had gotten dim, but not yet dark, so I left the porch and scrounged around the edges of the lawn until I found a slightly-bigger-than-my-fist rock. *That* would make more noise than my knuckles or a coin.

I picked the rock up and returned to the window.

Whap-whap-whap.

I had expected someone to yank open the curtain to investigate, but there was no reaction.

I adjusted my hold on the rock to make sure my fingers were clear of the largest side so I could bang harder and louder.

Thunk-thunk-thunk.

Nothing. The lively music continued to play. Nobody even came to tell me I'd be in serious trouble if I broke the glass.

Well, then . . . *All right, Emily. You asked for it.*

I left the porch again, to put more distance between me and the window. This time, I flung the rock with all my might.

Thump. Yikes!

I almost made it out of the way as the rock bounced off the window and shot right back at me. There was an unbelievable pain at my right temple . . .

. . . And the next thing I knew, I was coming to, sprawled on the grass, in such intense pain, I was convinced my head was split open and my brains were spilling out onto Emily's neatly trimmed lawn.

There isn't supposed to be pain in Rasmussem games. Discomfort, sure; that's part of the realism. But most of the games have players doing all sorts of dangerous things: swordfighting and facing down alien invasions and exploring haunted houses. Stuff most normal people wouldn't do in real life for fear of death and/or maiming. Rasmussem provides a safe way to have adventures. Who would pay to experience sword thrusts or laser burns or broken bones? I could only guess that the usual game protocols regarding pain hadn't been written in yet, or maybe the technicians assumed this world was too safe for its very young players to get hurt.

Gingerly, I touched my fingertips to my head. No great gaping wound, but definitely a nasty scrape—and that on top of a huge bump. I'd heard people refer to such a bump as a goose egg, but I'd never truly appreciated that term before.

Still, it was good news that the bump had had the time to grow to that prodigious size: time had obviously passed, and that gave a happier explanation for the darkness of my surroundings. It had been dusk when I'd been ejected from the dance, and I'd been worried that I'd hit myself so hard I'd started to go blind.

The candles were still flickering in the windows of Emily's house, excepting only the one with the drawn curtain, but there was no more music drifting out into the night. The musicians—and, I could only suppose, the beautiful women and the silent men—had gone home. Whatever home meant for game characters.

I couldn't tell how much time had passed. The sky was totally dark. Well, there were stars and a full moon, but no remnant of the setting sun or hint of a rising sun.

What had they made of my unconsciousness at Rasmussem? I suspected Mom would have demanded my return, yet again, if she'd realized what had happened, regardless of the official assurances of my safety. I could just imagine the scene back there: the secret glance that passed between Ms. Bennett and Adam when they realized what the flattened readouts meant, the silent mutual acknowledgment that they shouldn't say anything to Mom. They must have figured it would take less time for me to revive on my own than for them to fetch me back, hear me tell them that no, yet again I had nothing significant to report, and then have to return me to the game. Though Adam probably *had* made a note about it.

I sat up, and almost fell over sideways from the dizziness. So I sat there a few more minutes, listening to the chirp of the world's loudest nighttime peepers, my arms stretched out on either side, until I didn't feel so badly off balance. Fighting the urge to throw up, I struggled to my knees, then finally hauled myself to my feet.

My head still ached as though it might split open, but I

staggered back up onto the porch and once again rapped my knuckles against the window.

Tap.

The sound went right through me, though I was fairly certain I wasn't being as forceful as when I'd tried it earlier.

I went with one knuckle.

tap. tap. tap.

Each tap was like a smack across the top of my head. A smack with a piece of lumber.

But I didn't rouse anybody in the house.

Holding on to the rail because there was the very real danger of my tipping over, I made my way around the porch to the next window.

Tap, tap, tap, nothing.

Then the next: *Tap, tap, tap,* nothing.

Then I was at the French doors that opened from the kitchen. I'd forgotten about them.

Boy, I told myself, *I'll feel like a real pinhead if those turn out to be unlocked.*

My self-esteem remained intact in that regard: the doors were, in fact, Grace-proofed.

I sat down on the steps that led to the water, too dizzy to know if I was upset that I still couldn't get in or relieved that I hadn't inflicted my breaking-and-entering injury on myself pointlessly.

The water lapped against the dock, a noise that under normal circumstances would have been soothing. With my head aching the way it did, the sound felt more like metal garbage can lids clanging together.

Maybe I should go back to Rasmussem, I thought. Sure, I'd lose some time, but I could come back in a sound body. And I could tell Ms. Bennett she needed to fix the pain filters of this game. And I needed to tell her about the voiceless guys. Unquestionably they were some sort of clue. About something. Probably. Though, with my head throbbing, figuring things out was just too difficult. Besides, Emily was most likely asleep now. In Rasmussem games, you need to sleep just as surely as you do in real life. And if she hadn't wanted to talk to me when she'd been gathering flowers or dancing, she certainly wouldn't welcome being awakened in the dead of night.

Yet I kept coming back to the thought: the Rasmussem group hadn't brought me back when I'd knocked myself out, so they must consider a reset to be a waste of time.

The stars shone in the sky above, and reflected in the lake before me. I went to the water to dip my hands in, to cool my cheeks, not daring to put my fingers anywhere *near* my throbbing forehead.

The gondola was bobbing at the end of its tether, and despite the darkness, I could make out the shape of the gondolier standing in the bow—Prow? Which is the back?— patiently waiting to offer rides.

He was the only one here who had been nice to me.

I stood, still weaving a bit, and made my way down the

dock, my footsteps thudding against the wooden slats sounding like a herd of crazed wildebeests.

"*Buona notte,*" the gondolier greeted me. "*Le piacerebbe fare un giro in gondola?*"

Before I could tell him to please speak more softly, and that no, I did not want a ride in his stinking gondola, he took note of my bruised, bumped, and abraded forehead. He sucked in a breath through his teeth and made a sympathetic face as he brought his fingers to his own forehead and said in a kindly—if overly loud—voice, "*Che cosa è successo?*"

Our language differences didn't leave us too much common ground, but there was something I knew he understood. "Emily," I said.

"Emily," he said, once again kissing his fingertips to show his approval.

I tugged on his sleeve. "Emily," I repeated. "She's in trouble."

Well, she was.

I pointed back to the house.

"Emily. She needs help." I indicated my head, as though what had happened to me might—without his intervention—happen to her, too. "Emily. Help."

Whatever he made of my words, he understood my frantic tone. Nimbly, he leaped onto the dock and strode toward the house.

I followed as quickly as my pounding head permitted.

He'd already tried the French doors by the time I got

there. He knocked, very loudly—oh, my aching head—very, very loudly. He pounded the flat of his palm against the wood, shaking the door in its frame, and called in that deep, serious voice guys can do: "*Signorina* Emily!"

"*Andiamo*," I told him, the word rising to the surface of my brain from who-knows-where—probably some movie or song or Italian restaurant or something. I was fairly certain it meant something along the lines of "Let's get going" or "Hurry up." I repeated it more urgently: "*Andiamo! Andiamo!* Emily!"

He put his shoulder to the door and tried to crash through it the way cops do in the movies. But whatever Emily's doors and windows were made of, the door didn't break, and he bounced off the surface as surely as that rock I'd thrown.

Leaping off the porch, he stood on the lawn and bellowed up at the second floor, "*Signorina* Emily!" over and over, until finally my sister opened the wooden shutters of her room and stepped out onto the balcony.

She was wearing a floaty white nightgown that made her look simultaneously romantic and little-girlish.

I wanted to tell her, "Emily, I'm here to rescue you. I've brought reinforcements." But I didn't know if that was the right thing to say, so I didn't say anything. Besides, I was intentionally standing close to the huge flowering cherry tree, kind of hoping that she wouldn't notice me, since my presence seemed to irk her.

In a voice that belied her sweet, vulnerable appearance, Emily shouted at the gondolier, "Go away!" She saw me there, too, despite the tree. She added, "Go away, both of you!" and stomped back into her room, slamming the shutters closed.

Angry, but undeterred, I thought at her: *Well, this is what you get for not letting your guys speak English.* To the gondolier, I said, "Emily!" and pointed up to where she'd been, then pointed to my head. "She needs our help! *Andiamo!*"

I don't know what he thought was going on, but clearly my insistence was convincing him that Emily needed rescuing and she needed it *now*.

Which was true enough, just probably not the way he thought.

He looked around, then climbed up onto the porch rail, and from there hoisted himself up into the cherry tree, whose upper branches came fairly close to her balcony.

Uh, wait a minute, I thought. I couldn't follow him that way.

"Ahm . . ." I called after him as he climbed up and up. I had been counting on his forcing his way in through either the front or back door, or on our being annoying enough that Emily would come out. His gaining access to her room via the tree wouldn't help me at all.

"*Signorina* Emily!" the gondolier called again. The

branches that would support his weight were not all that close to the window, so he took a flying leap.

"Careful," I whisper-warned him.

And he landed lightly on the balcony rail, then jumped down to the balcony itself. I guess a gondolier does have to have good equilibrium. Maybe somehow this would work after all. Maybe Emily would realize I couldn't be ignored.

The gondolier kicked in the wooden shutters.

I heard Emily yell, "Guards!"

"Emily!" I called, though my head pounded in protest.

So I don't know if the gondolier said anything as he swayed there, holding on to the window frame for support and balance. Or if Emily did. What I *saw* was the gondolier stagger backwards, shoved by someone in the room. A guy who could have been the same one who threw me out of the dance strode out onto the balcony. I saw the guy grab hold of the gondolier.

Pick him up off his feet.

High off his feet.

And toss him over the rail.

This was so unexpected, so unreal, I thought, *He'll land on his feet back on the branch he jumped from*—like a scene from a cartoon, run backwards for comic effect.

But he didn't land on that branch.

At least, not on his feet.

And he certainly didn't land *only* on that branch.

He hit several as he fell, fell, fell, before his body finally landed in a crumpled heap on the ground. I went running up to him, but I didn't need to. I already knew there was no way anyone could have survived that fall.

Okay, he was only a computer-generated character, but he had been kind to me. And he had been concerned about Emily. Emily, who might well have helped to program him so that all he knew was gondoliering and being loyal to her; Emily, who now poked her head out beyond the jagged edges of the window shutter and called down to me, "Go away, Grace. I don't want you here." She wasn't shocked, she wasn't rattled, she wasn't acting like "Oh no, this is not what I intended."

I had thought before that she wasn't the same Emily I knew. Now I had no idea who she was.

She closed—as best she could—what was left of the shutters, leaving her guard out on the balcony, still watching me with those cold, bland eyes looking out from his pretty face.

Suddenly, I didn't want to be here, either, couldn't bear to be here. "End game," I announced to the eavesdropping Rasmussem personnel. "Bring me back to Rasmussem." And I sat down on the grass among the fragrant cherry blossoms that had been knocked loose as the gondolier fell, and I waited to be brought back home.

CHAPTER 9

Fun and Games with Phones

W HEN I TOLD everyone what Emily's dance partner/ bodyguard/hit man had done to the gondolier, Ms. Bennett said, "Nothing like that should be able to happen."

Mom whirled on her and snapped, "Do you listen to yourself? Do you have any idea how often you have said that?"

I saw the flash of irritation on Ms. Bennett's face. But she didn't lash out. She simply changed the topic and asked me for more details about what I'd seen at the dance.

Mom cut me off, demanding instead, "Grace, are you all right?"

I realized I was sitting there on the total immersion couch with my hand feeling my forehead. It wasn't that my head still hurt from that rebounding rock, but it shouldn't have hurt in the game, either, not that intensely, and that was yet one more thing Ms. Bennett had said simply shouldn't happen.

"I think," I said, making a conscious effort to put my

hands in my lap, "we really need to get in contact with Frank Lupiano."

Adam grunted but pretended he was caught up in studying the computer readouts from those minutes I'd just spent in the game.

"What are you thinking?" Mom asked me.

I didn't want to hurt her, but I didn't want us to miss something because I'd tried to spare her feelings.

"Surely," I said, "it can't be . . ." Hmm, what was the word I was looking for? *Normal? Right? Healthy?* I veered and approached from a slightly different angle. "It can't be a coincidence that all the guys in Emily's world either don't speak English, or don't speak at all?"

Ms. Bennett said, "So you suspect . . . ?"

Suspect was too active a verb. "So I'm wondering . . . I don't know . . . maybe something happened with Frank. A fight? Maybe she doesn't want to hear what guys have to say because she's mad at him."

Mom glared at Adam, who—for the moment, in this room, anyway—represented all guys in all their reprehensible breaking-daughters'-hearts ways.

Ms. Bennett said, "We've been trying to reach this Frank ever since your mother gave us his name."

"How?" I asked.

Although she looked puzzled about why I was questioning that, she answered, "Your sister's phone. We got the number from her contact list, but he hasn't been answering."

"Which he might not," I pointed out, "if you've been using her phone and they had a fight."

Ms. Bennett nodded, even as she said, "But we left a voice mail, and tried texting him, too."

"From *her* phone," I repeated. It almost made more sense than switching to a land line. That way, they could keep hitting redial.

Unfortunately, that was just the way a jilted girlfriend might think. Not that I'd ever done that. But I might have considered it. Once. With a particular seventh-grade boy I have long since realized I was lucky to be rid of.

"Still," Adam was saying, "I identified myself as being from Rasmussem and said that there was an emergency with Emily and that we needed to talk to him."

"Adam," I said, suddenly feeling like I was the one with experience and he was the little kid. "Like a certain kind of ticked-off girl wouldn't text something exactly like that if she was being ignored?"

I could tell by their faces that they saw I was right. Even Mom.

"Call from the phone in my office," Ms. Bennett instructed Adam.

"Too late," I said. "He might not pick up if he doesn't recognize the incoming number."

"What do you recommend, Grace?" Ms. Bennett asked me.

"A call he can't ignore . . ."

"The police?" Mom asked.

"Mom! No."

My thinking was *Too much time trying to explain.* But Ms. Bennett wore a horrified look, and I'm guessing that she was thinking *Too much opportunity for a publicity leak.*

I suggested, "Announce yourselves as being from Stoney's Barbeque Pit. You know how they have that promotion going: 'Answer your phone or call us back in five minutes, and win a barbeque feast for you and four of your friends.' "

"Misrepresent ourselves on the phone?" Ms. Bennett asked. But in another moment she told Adam, "Do it."

I said, "But Adam already left a voice message. Frank might recognize his voice. It might be better if you did this."

Ms. Bennett said, "Do I sound like a Barbeque Pit sort of gal?" She sighed but started for the door.

"Should we be there?" I called after her. "Just in case?"

"Just in case what?"

Just in case you try something—I don't know what, but the truth is I don't fully trust you, since you have Emily's best interests at heart only so long as they don't clash with Rasmussem's best interests.

But while I was trying to figure out a slightly more diplomatic answer, she gave a wave of her hand that we took to mean *All right, come on.*

I hopped off the total immersion couch and followed her down the hall, not taking the time to put my sneakers back on. My mother walked next to me, holding my hand, which I knew looked three levels beyond pathetic, but I wasn't going to be the one to tell her that, even when we walked past a bunch of cubicles where employees glanced up at us from their computers. Behind Ms. Bennett's back, a pair of women at a water cooler motioned for Adam to join them. He obviously didn't dare risk having Ms. Bennett notice that he'd fallen behind, and shook his head.

Ms. Bennett, it turned out, was important enough that she had a real office, with regular walls and a door. When she opened that door, we all saw Sybella sitting at the desk, talking on Emily's cell phone. True, she'd been told to check Emily's contacts. But we all instinctively knew it was not good to get caught actually parking herself in the boss's chair: Sybella got her skinny little butt out of there even before Ms. Bennett crossed her arms and gave her what kids around the world recognize as The Look.

"No, never mind," Sybella said, wrapping up her conversation from a standing position. "Sorry to bother you." She snapped the phone shut and explained the call rather than the reasoning behind making herself at home in the big cheese's office furniture. "JoAnn's. As in the craft store, not a close personal friend named Joann."

"She wanted to work there last summer," Mom explained. "They said to keep calling to see if there was an opening, but there never was."

"Which explains why nobody there knew her," Sybella said. Glancing at me, but speaking to Ms. Bennett, she asked, "So, any breakthroughs?"

Ms. Bennett held her hand out for the phone and looked up Frank's number, which she wrote down. Then she handed Emily's phone back to Sybella and said, "You can go through the rest of Emily's contact list in the conference room," proof that she still figured Sybella was an irritant to Mom, even if Mom was willing to speak to her.

Sybella left, and Ms. Bennett reclaimed her desk. She took a deep breath, dialed Frank's number, and put on an enormous smile, which she kept through what must have been three rings and a prompt to leave a message. "Hi!" she said in a voice that had developed a sudden hint of Texas— which, I guess, the thought of smoked ribs and beef brisket tends to bring out in people. "This is Cheryl-Anne, from Stoney's Barbeque—home of the Fabulous Finger-Lickin' Mouth-Watering Stoney's Platter for Five. And you, lucky contestant, have had your number selected—"

By her abrupt stop, we could tell Frank had gone for the barbeque bait and had answered the phone.

"Listen up," Ms. Bennett said, all trace of Cheryl-Anne from Stoney's gone, replaced with a hard edge that was also new to us. "I'm Dr. Jenna Bennett, chief technical engineer at Rasmussem Corporation, and if you hang up, representatives from the Rochester Police Department will be going to your home to bring your mother in for questioning. I'm assuming she won't be pleased about that, so you consider well, young man."

I could hear Frank's voice seeping out of the receiver, loud and angry, but I couldn't make out what he was saying.

That was probably all for the best.

"No, this is *not* a prank. If you hang up, this *will* become a matter for the police."

After giving him all of about a heartbeat to think this over, she continued. "Your girlfriend, Emily Pizzelli, has gotten herself into some very serious trouble, and we want to know what insight you can give us into her state of mind. When was the last time you spoke with her?"

A pause, with Frank's tinny voice telling her something.

"Since when?" Ms. Bennett asked. Then she demanded, "Tell me the circumstances." Then, "It stopped being personal when Emily took it upon herself to do what she did, about which I cannot be more specific because (a) there's no time, and (b) I don't have clearance from our legal department, and (c) the opportunity for that will be when criminal charges are made."

Having seen Ms. Bennett put on the convincing persona of Cheryl-Anne from Stoney's, it was hard for me to judge how real that threat was.

Frank, however, was apparently convinced and spilling his guts.

"So," Ms. Bennett said after a short bit, "not an amicable separation."

I glanced at Mom, who looked grim. I probably did, too. I had come to suspect this, from what I had seen in the game, but until then, we had all assumed Emily and Frank were a happy couple.

Ms. Bennett said, "All right, Frank, I need you to keep in mind that a young woman's life literally hangs in the balance. Is there anything else you're not telling me?" She angled her chair away from us. Clearly, she didn't want us to see her face—or maybe it was that she didn't want to see ours. She asked Frank, "Could she be pregnant?"

I heard Mom gasp, felt her grip on my fingers tighten, but she didn't protest.

Ms. Bennett was shaking her head, either to reassure Mom or at something Frank was saying. "It better be," she said. "It better be the truth. And if I call you again, young man, you'd better pick up."

She hung up the phone and swung back to face us. "He says no." We didn't need to ask which part of the conversation she was talking about. To my mom, she added, "I had to ask."

"I understand," Mom squeaked.

"He says that they grew apart," Ms. Bennett told us.

"That she became needy and clingy, and demanded constant reassurance."

"That doesn't sound like her," Mom protested.

"None of this does," I pointed out. Flower-matching games and princess dresses and more pink than in a whole case of Pepto-Bismol? Refusing to talk to me? Killing off loyal game characters when, even at eighteen years old, she *still* had to fast-forward the movie when it got to the part where Bambi's mother gets shot? No, this most definitely did not sound like Emily.

"Agreed," Ms. Bennett said, though obviously she was just guessing, or saying what she figured we wanted to hear. She couldn't *know*, not the way we did. "Grace," she said, "are you willing to go back, armed with this new knowledge?"

"Wait a minute," Mom said. "So Emily and her boyfriend break up, and that makes Emily so depressed she decides to go into a fantasy game and not come out?"

"It's the closest thing we have to a theory," Ms. Bennett said.

I'd almost forgotten Adam, because he'd come in behind us and hadn't said a word; but now he cleared his throat and said, "Well, I guess that would sort of explain . . ."

He hesitated, and Mom snapped, "What? What would it explain?"

I didn't think grown guys could blush, but he did. "Well . . . the way . . . she . . . sort of . . . came on to me."

"Oh for goodness' sakes!" Mom said.

Emily? I thought. *Popular, happy Emily, who has to practically beat boys off with a stick? She put the moves on Adam?*

But then I thought, *She could have had just about any guy in high school, but she chose Frank. And now it turns out Frank is a weasel.*

I suspected Adam was a bit of a weasel himself.

But that wasn't the point.

Ms. Bennett scowled at Adam. "You might have mentioned this before."

"I didn't think it was relevant," he protested. "I explained to her that I'm engaged, and that was the end of it."

That wasn't the point, either. The point was: if Emily had her heart broken by a boy, shouldn't she want sisterly companionship and compassion?

I said, "So I'm supposed to . . . what? Go in there and tell her 'You're better off without him'? 'There are other fish in the sea'? 'There's someone you're destined to meet, and he's not here in this game'?"

"It's a starting point," Ms. Bennett said.

"How about this, instead?" I suggested. "If she's retreating into this made-up world because she likes that better than the real world . . ." I spared a moment to mentally add,

Though God knows why, because I can't see it, with or without Frank's being a worm, not to get my mammals and inverte-brates confused or anything. ". . . why don't we alter the world we can?"

Mom said, "What?"

"Get rid of her perfect setting. Program a cold, rainy day. Give her blight in her garden, termites in the wood-work of the house, guys who can't stop talking—about themselves. I don't know . . . dust, mildew, allergens, a plague of locusts. Make the game world less appealing."

Ms. Bennett was nodding. "Yes," she said. "We tried that."

Now it was my turn to be confused. I hadn't seen any of those things.

Adam explained, "She modified the code to shut us out. So, yeah, we programmed things like that—we wrote out the sprites so she couldn't have any more wishes, we made the weather hot and muggy, we inserted a next-door neighbor in a trailer who tuned up his motorcycle engine all day long and played German opera at full volume all night. None of those things showed up. She put in a buffer to de-lay us. *She* can change things immediately from within the game, but any updates *we* put in won't take effect for an-other seventy-two hours."

And Emily didn't have seventy-two hours. They didn't need to tell us that. We didn't know how long Emily had before the equipment—meant to be used for under an hour—would overheat her brain. In Principal Overstreet's office, Ms. Bennett had said Emily had already been hooked up for more than four hours. I suspected Ms. Bennett and Mr. Kroll might have been downplaying the elapsed time so that Mom and I wouldn't panic, and that "more than four hours" might mean "a lot more." But even if it was exactly four back then at school, by now it was closer to six. Maybe it would be another two or three hours before the equipment would cause irreversible brain damage. Maybe a bit longer. But the time Emily had left was definitely less than seventy-two hours.

It was hard to concentrate with a deadline like that looming over us. *Don't panic*, I had to tell myself. I couldn't be any use to Emily if my brain froze.

Adam finished apologetically, apparently knowing how lame he sounded, "We've got people working on trying to eliminate that buffer."

So much for my brilliant ingenuity saving the day.

"Which brings us back to Grace," Ms. Bennett said. "Grace, are you willing to reenter the game and talk to your sister about her love life?"

Before I could say okay, Mom suggested, "Maybe it should be me?"

We just looked at her.

Mom picked up on our skepticism. "What?" she said.

"Let Grace give it another try," Ms. Bennett told her. "Parents tend to put kids on the defensive. Emily might be more open with her sister than with her mother." To me, Ms. Bennett added, "Grace, that was good work you did, finding that lead about the boyfriend. See what else you can learn."

It wasn't that Emily and I had had many conversations of the deep, meaningful variety, not given the difference in our ages, but I had to think Ms. Bennett had a point about the likelihood of Emily being willing to tell all to Mom. Besides, the idea of Mom tromping through the game universe—dealing with malicious sprites and vicious bodyguards, figuring out the magic, having to determine what was important and what was just mundane game stuff—that was enough to cause *my* brain to overheat.

"I'll try it again," I said.

CHAPTER 10

In the Woods

W E'LL WORK on that pain filter," Adam told me, once we were back in the total immersion room—which might have been more reassuring if they hadn't already explained about that buffer where any changes had a seventy-two-hour lag before going into effect.

With my newfound bossiness, I took control of the one thing I could. I screwed up my assertiveness and announced, "I am not counting backwards from a hundred by sevens."

Turns out, this was a big deal only to me. "Fine," Ms Bennett said as Adam attached the leads to my temples.

Prepared for an argument, I said. "Oh. Okay." Then I said, "What should I count back by?"

"Whatever you want," Ms. Bennett said. "Or nothing at all."

Lying there staring at the insides of my eyelids, I found that time crawled by. I suddenly realized that the mathematics was to keep my mind from spinning off in alarming directions. "One hundred," I said. "Ninety-three . . ."

What with my slow start, that was pretty much all I had time for.

I felt the shift in the quality of the air and opened my eyes.

I had gotten so used to the Victorian house, the garden, and the lake, I'd lost track of that path of crushed sparkly stones that led into the woods. But I was in the woods now.

Specifically, I was lying down in a tent in the woods. And by *tent* I do not mean anything like what the Boy Scouts of America camp out in. This was a pavilion, its sides of white silk billowing prettily in the breeze, which was how I could see the trees beyond. Several sets of wind chimes— some silver-belled, some made with brass tubes, and one of dried bamboo—struck random musical notes that would have been soothing if they didn't remind me of the sprites.

The pavilion was about as big as our living room. No furnishings that I could see, at least not from my current position. But there was a treasure chest, overflowing with both jewels and jewelry. That made me suspect that the tent poles—which looked like gold—probably really *were* gold. From the umbrella-like scaffolding that held up the ceiling hung a large wicker cage, which housed a happy little songbird that was chirping away. Satin pillows were strewn about the ground for sitting on; I myself was lying on a hammock with its own pillows, so it was very comfortable, and it swayed gently, a very relaxing motion.

The only bit of unpleasantness was a sour, musty smell, like old sweat. Oh, wait. That was me.

Now that I was back in this world, my head once again ached from where the stone had hit me. Time had passed in the game since the events of the night before, so the computer program assumed that I would have begun healing. But only a little. I touched my forehead and found a bump, but it was no longer so big that it felt as though a full-grown squirrel were about to burst out of there. So that was *some* progress.

I suspected the headache wouldn't get better from sitting up. My head, the breeze, the wind chimes, the twittering of the bird, the swaying of the hammock, all conspired to make me reluctant to move, though I knew I'd have to, and that sooner would be better than later for Emily, if not for my head.

Knowing there's a way to get out of a hammock, but not knowing what that way is, I managed to sit up, bracing my elbows on the rope edges. While I sat there for a moment, wondering what my next move should be, a glittery butterfly landed on the back of my right hand with a faint, not unpleasant tickle.

Afraid to lose my balance by moving too much, I simply flipped my hand over. Obligingly, the butterfly shifted to my palm, and I closed my fingers, where I felt it turn, solid and cold, into a coin.

I really need to get moving, I thought. *I really need to look for Emily.*

The memory of how uninterested she had been in seeing me, much less in being rescued by me, added to my distrust of my ability to get out of the hammock without seriously injuring myself.

Until I noticed an extra limb.

Well, an extra hand, to be exact.

Not attached to me, which was good no matter how you look at it, but, still, holding on to the edge of the hammock. Gently tugging on the hammock, which explained the swaying motion. Given that I wasn't on a boat, I should have realized that *needed* explaining.

The hand was attached to an arm; the arm was attached to a handsome young man; the handsome young man was kneeling beside the hammock, about level with my head, smiling tenderly at me.

A smile just like those of the guys last night. Before they threw me out of the dance and tossed the gondolier to his death from the balcony window.

I yelped. And half fell out of the hammock trying to get away from him, except that he deftly caught me.

"Get away from me!" I cried, swatting at his hands.

He did, once my feet were firmly settled on the ground.

The moving I had done and the sound of my own voice got my head throbbing again. I shoved the butterfly coin into the pocket of my by-now-badly-bedraggled dress as I glanced around for something with which to defend myself. I had pretty much seen all there was to see from the hammock. I could beat the guy with a pillow or with the birdcage, or I could try strangling him with a pearl necklace from the treasure chest, maybe stab him with a brooch.

But except for the fact that he was smiling so kindly it made my skin crawl, the guy wasn't doing anything. He remained on his knees, as though ready to rock me in the hammock for as long as the game lasted.

"Stay," I ordered him.

And fortunately, he stayed.

I backed away, outside.

The guy remained, waiting for someone—anyone, apparently—to come in to be rocked in the hammock.

The tent was in a clearing from which two sparkle-stoned paths led in two different directions. Neither one seemed any better than the other, so I pulled the coin out of my pocket and told myself, *Butterfly side, I'll go to the left; Rasmussem logo, I'll go right.* I flipped the coin and headed left.

Presumably, Emily was in the area. Or had been, when Adam and Ms. Bennett had made their calculations. I walked and walked and walked—which, trust me, was no fun with one bare foot. I was just wondering whether the Rasmussem people would pull me back to headquarters if I wandered too far from where Emily was, when I saw that I was coming to another clearing. The trees were thinning, and I could see a block of color—pinkish-purple—that indicated a building up ahead.

But a few more steps and I realized that what I was seeing was the back of the Victorian house.

I stopped. Sighed loudly. But of course there was nobody nearby to hear my exasperation.

Obviously, if Emily had been at the house or on the lake, I would have been set down in the gazebo, as I had been the other times. All the other times.

And then I remembered that Emily probably wouldn't be on the lake—not unless she was willing to paddle the gondola herself. Though, maybe, with her stash of butterfly coins and the sprites granting her wishes, she could just whip herself up a new gondolier.

I wasn't curious enough to go around to the other side to see; I turned and headed back down the path I'd just come along. Down the path, down the path, past (eventually) the pavilion, where I took the right-hand path.

It was only a few more minutes before I could hear music being played. Not like the chamber music at the dance the night before, but a single instrument, played calm and slow and sweet. *Lute*, I found myself thinking, though I wasn't sure, not really, what a lute sounded like. This was sort of like a cross between a guitar and a harp.

A few more steps, and I was at another clearing.

This one had a guy in it, sitting on a stool, playing a musical instrument. Seeing the actual instrument, I was no closer than before to knowing what it was. Something with strings and a long skinny neck—the instrument, not the guy.

The guy was dressed in tunic and tights, clothing that made me think we were several centuries earlier than the night before, with its seventeen-hundreds-type finery. He more closely resembled the hammock-rocking man, though I'd been too afraid of him to take much note of his clothing.

It was only after taking in and thinking all those things that I noticed Emily was there, too. She was sitting on the ground, beneath a tree at the opposite end of the clearing.

And lying there, with its head on her lap, was a unicorn.

Emily was wearing a white dress asparkle with silver threads, and she had a Renaissance-Faire-type flowers-and-ribbons wreath on her head. Her eyes were closed and she was stroking the unicorn's head, both of them wearing looks that said *This is contentment. I could do this forever.*

But then the unicorn looked up as my feet took me actually into the clearing. It made a noise, not exactly a horse's whinny, but what I guess must have been the unicorn equivalent: softer, gentler than a horse, maybe with the hint of a kitten's purr to it.

Emily opened her eyes and groaned. "Can't you stop following me?" she asked. "Isn't it enough that you ruined the house for me?"

I was somewhat relieved to hear that the gondolier's messy death *had* ruined her enjoyment of the house.

Maybe her heart hadn't turned to stone after all.

She just acted that way toward me.

While we'd been talking, lute-guy continued strumming, but the unicorn gracefully got to its feet and came toward me. It put its head down, almost a bow. The way things were going, I half suspected its intent was to impale me, but all it did was nudge me. Again, sort of like a cat, demanding to be petted. I put my hand on its forelock, and immediately my headache—in fact, all my aches and pains—disappeared, healed by its touch.

Too bad, I thought, *it evidently can't heal what's ailing Emily.*

I said, "Ms. Bennett talked to Frank."

"Frank," Emily said, "is a pimple on the butt of humanity."

"Yes," I agreed.

"You don't know anything about it."

It seemed she was in the mood to argue about everything.

Be like that, I thought. What I said was "If you don't want to talk to me, do you want me to bring one of your friends? I'm sure any one of them would be willing to come here—"

"I don't have any friends," Emily interrupted.

"Of course you do."

"Don't make me get mean to you," she warned.

"*Get* mean?" I started to laugh. I couldn't help it. Maybe—ever so slightly—I was veering toward hysteria.

Emily stood. Emily raised her hands to the sky.

Emily turned into a dragon.

The dragon shot a blast of flame at me.

A moment before the flame hit, I thought, *I bet that unicorn won't be able to heal this.*

CHAPTER 11

Friends

I AM GETTING SICK and tired of this," I announced, even before my eyes opened. On the other hand, death by dragon must have been something the Rasmussem people *had* anticipated might happen: very fortunately I had immediately gone into the fizziness that's the Rasmussem equivalent of dying rather than actually experiencing what it's like to be flame-roasted by a dragon.

"What happened?" Mom asked.

I spared her the specifics. Well, no. To be honest: I spared *myself* the specifics. You know you've put yourself in a bad situation when you can say: *Thank goodness all that happened was I died.*

"Emily doesn't have any friends," I told her, told Ms. Bennett and Adam.

"Of course she does," Mom said, just what I'd tried to tell Emily before . . . before . . .

With those wonky pain filters not up to full speed, the thought of what I *might* have felt—a human campfire marshmallow—was not one on which my mind wanted to linger.

Adam said, "The people we've been reaching on her phone—they've all identified themselves as being friends from high school. Nobody from college."

"Nobody?" Mom sounded as incredulous as I felt.

Adam didn't bother repeating. He finished, "And most of them haven't heard from her since summer."

"That's . . ." Mom started, but she didn't know how to finish her thought any better than I did.

I said, "What about what's-her-name? Her roommate?" I wasn't trying to be cute—I was honestly blanking out. We had met Emily's assigned roommate that first day. Our family/her family: we kept getting in one another's way unloading cars, trying to cram about twice as much into the dorm room as it was physically capable of holding. The girl had muddy-blond hair and an accent my dad had immediately recognized from his travels—What was it? Rhode Island? Connecticut?—despite the fact . . . "Ooo," I said, "I remember: She was named after one of those western states. Dakota?"

My mother gave me a how-did-I-ever-come-to-spawn-you look. "Georgia," she corrected me. She asked Ms. Bennett, "Are you sure that equipment of yours isn't damaging Grace's brain?"

"Nope," Ms. Bennett said. "That would be the New York State educational system."

I took that to mean that either Dakota or Georgia wasn't one of those western states.

In any case, I was realizing that on her visits home, Emily hadn't talked much about her roommate. Now that I thought about it, she hadn't talked much about anybody at all. She'd just say "the girls in the dorm" or "someone from my sociology class."

Adam pressed a couple of buttons on his hand-held, then shook his head. "Your mother gave us a few names before we picked you up from school. Georgia Chappell was one of them. She hasn't returned our call."

Ms. Bennett said, "Tell Sybella she should switch to the land line and give all the no-answers on Emily's contact list a second try, just in case."

Just in case. I knew she meant that Frank Lupiano might not be the only supposed friend who was screening his calls to avoid Emily.

I asked, "What about Danielle Gardner?" Danielle was Emily's best friend—had been since middle school. As good as Emily was with computers, that's how good Danielle was with artsy things like textile design. They had planned to go to RIT together. And even though they would have been in different programs, they were going to apply to be room-mates. But Danielle hadn't been accepted at RIT. She'd been put on the waiting list and told to reapply in January. I remembered Emily explaining to Mom and Dad that a lot of students would drop out after the first semester, and that

Danielle was sure to get in and should take some of the basic requirements at MCC, the community college, so that the two of them could still graduate together in four years. I remembered Dad asking, "So is that what Danielle's going to do?" and Emily answering, "I guess."

I guess. That was pretty vague for best friends. And hard as I thought about it, I didn't have an end for that story—happy or otherwise. It was only at this moment that I realized we hadn't seen much of Danielle over the summer. Now it was March, and I simply couldn't remember ever hearing Emily say whether Danielle had followed her advice about MCC for the fall semester or—more important—whether she'd been accepted at RIT in January.

Adam had been checking his hand-held. He nodded at Mom. "That was another of the names you gave us, but it wasn't on Emily's contact list."

Mom repeated the name: "Danielle Gardner. Yes, if anybody will know what's going on . . ."

But Adam was shaking his head. "No Danielle. No Gardner."

Mom said, "Well . . . Emily wouldn't need to have the number on her list. She'd know it by heart."

I may have mentioned Mom is not real good at technology. I told her, "It'd be on her speed dial." A glance at Adam showed it wasn't.

Mom said, "Mrs. Gardner—Tanya—she has her own business, doing sewing alterations at home, so she should be at the house. I'll talk to her," and she held her hand out for the phone.

One ring, two. I could tell when Danielle's mom picked up by the way my mother stood taller.

"Tanya, this is Marilyn Pizzelli, Emily's mother . . . Yes, yes, it has been a while . . . Well, no, actually not . . ." Mom made a *Come on, wrap it up* gesture with her hand, even though we were the only ones who could see it. Finally, forcefully, probably interrupting, she said, "Tanya." She took a deep breath. "Something serious has come up with Emily, and we're hoping Danielle can help. Is she home from school yet?" Mom looked confused. "Oh," she said, "I was under the impression she was staying at home and going to MCC . . . No . . . No, I didn't realize that . . ." She rolled her eyes. "I'm very pleased she got into Geneseo . . . Yes, I know it's a good school . . . Tanya, I really need to talk to Danielle—it's urgent. Could you please give me her phone number?"

Ms. Bennett was making gestures like semaphore flags with her hands. "Residence Advisor," she mouthed.

I knew that was in case Danielle didn't pick up and needed to be tracked down on campus.

Geneseo? I thought. What was Danielle doing going to Geneseo, instead of RIT with Emily?

Mom wrote down both phone numbers and finally managed to end the conversation with the talkative Mrs. Gardner. I could see her hand shaking.

"You did fine," Ms. Bennett said, but she took the phone to make the call to Danielle herself.

Sure, I thought, thinking of how she had spoken to Frank, *scare the hell out of the poor girl.*

But they hadn't had Danielle's number before, as opposed to her not answering—so Ms. Bennett didn't go all legal and ballistic when Danielle answered.

She also—I could tell—didn't get anywhere with her.

When she hung up, after several "If-you-think-of-anything's," she told us, "She says she doesn't know why her number isn't on Emily's list, and suggests maybe it got erased accidentally." She made a *How-likely-is-that?* face before continuing, "But in any case, she says they talk two or three times a week. On the other hand, she also says Emily never said anything about a fight with Frank Lupiano. She hasn't noticed any unusual behavior with Emily, has no idea what could be troubling her."

Adam pulled out his phone and dialed a number. "Sybella," he said, "can you check Emily's phone for calls made and calls received? Look for this number . . ."

Ms. Bennett turned the clipboard so that he could read Danielle's phone number.

After a few moments, he said, "Did you check both voice and text? Okay. How far back does the record go? Thanks." He snapped his phone shut and gave a triumphant grin. "No calls to or from that number," he said. "And Emily's log goes back as far as November."

"Did I," Ms. Bennett asked, "or did I not make it clear to that little . . . young lady . . . that this was very important?" She held out her hand for Adam to return the phone.

"You made it clear," Mom said. But she was obviously shaken that Emily's best friend was covering something. "Why would Danielle lie?" Mom asked me. Like I would have some special insight. "After all the times she ate over, and slept over, the times we brought her with us to Darien Lake and treated her like family?"

"I don't know," I said. I might have suggested that maybe Danielle misunderstood and somehow thought she was doing Emily a favor by covering for her, but I had heard Ms. Bennett tell her, "I don't want to sound overly dramatic, but her very life is in danger." I mean, if someone said that to me about my best friend, I would have spilled my guts.

And that didn't explain why they hadn't called each other in months.

This time, the phone rang once, then went straight to voice mail.

Next, Ms. Bennett called Danielle's dorm adviser, where she had to leave a message. I don't think I'd ever heard anyone say "important," "urgent," and "of gravest consequence" so often in one headache-inducing sentence.

"I'll call Tanya Gardner again," Mom said when Ms. Bennett finally hung up, sounding angry now. "I'll tell her that her daughter is endangering—"

Ms. Bennett was shaking her head. "We've tried this on our own. I think it's time to call in the police."

That was scary, since I could be sure Rasmussem's legal department, as embodied by Mr. Kroll, would have warned against the bad publicity of a police report.

"Campus security would be more likely than city police to be able to find her," Adam pointed out, "knowing the layout of the college."

"Campus cops are no more scary than mall cops," Ms. Bennett countered. "I want someone to scare this girl to a point just short of cardiac arrest."

"Maybe I should drive to Geneseo to try to talk to her," Mom said. "Explain. It's only about forty-five minutes away. Surely if I just explained—"

"Send me back," I interrupted.

That *did* quiet the room.

"There's no time for all this," I said. "Send me back."

"Are you sure?" Ms. Bennett asked. By the readouts she and Adam had been monitoring, she had no doubt seen exactly what had happened to me—how I had left the game that last time.

"She has no friends," I said—what I had said before, when I'd been simply repeating Emily's words. But this time, I meant: *If not me, who?*

I asked, "Is this transforming-into-a-dragon thing part of the game?"

"Dragon?" Mom asked.

"Yes," Ms. Bennett said. "But having the ability to turn into a dragon means she's paid lots of money to the sprites."

"Dragon?" Mom repeated.

Adam added, "She's altered the game to make getting coins a lot easier. She's going to be hard to fight, if she's in a fighting mood."

"Yeah," I said, "well, she's put me in a fighting mood, too. And I have a plan."

CHAPTER 12

The Plan

I ENTERED THE Land of the Golden Butterflies right where I'd asked Ms. Bennett and Adam to set me down—in the pavilion—even though Adam had pointed out, "She's nowhere near there anymore. She's moved to a different area entirely."

"That's fine," I'd assured them. "I'll be able to find her." I hadn't added out loud what I'd been thinking: *I hope.*

So there I was, watching the white silk tent billow in the breeze, listening to the wind chimes, while gently rocking in a hammock that I now knew was smiling-guy-propelled. The treasure chest overflowing with the golden and sparkly goodies Emily had accumulated was still there.

One of the shimmery butterflies that were always nearby when I entered the game landed on my arm. I wouldn't need coins, not if my plan worked.

But since when could I count on my plans working? I captured the butterfly and put the resulting coin with the others in my pocket.

Then, finally, I turned my head to bring hammock-guy into view.

Yep, still there. Still handsome. Still smiling.

Okay, so he might as well be useful.

"Give me a hand up out of here?" I asked.

He did, steadying both me and the hammock.

"Thank you," I said. "Can you pick up that treasure chest?"

He did that, too, though he grunted at its weight.

"Follow me," I said.

The two of us walked—well, one of us walked, the other staggered under his load—down the path of crushed glittery stones that led off to the left, toward the Victorian house.

I ended up sending him ahead of me, as the chest was too full for the lid to close, and we were leaving a trail of gems, and golden plates and goblets, and strands of pearls. Sort of like Hansel and Gretel dropping bread crumbs—but in the *More Money Than Brains* edition.

By the time we got to the garden, hammock-guy was puffing and sweating. Obviously, toting a chest overflowing with Emily's accumulated riches was a lot more strenuous than what a hammock-swaying specialist guy was used to. But his aim was to please, and he pleased me as long as he was willing to haul. I did let him rest on one of the park benches for a couple of minutes, but I was antsy to get moving again. So I asked, "All right?" and he nodded. I suspected he had been programmed to happily agree to any request, even if his heart was about to burst from the physical exertion, but I didn't let that worry me.

I led him into the maze.

I probably should have asked him if he knew the shortest route to the sprite fountain, because I took us to several dead ends. But eventually, over the huffing of hammock-guy, I heard the sound of the sprites' laughter. And it only took two more dead ends before we found the clearing in the center of the maze.

There were two sprites, one sitting on the head of the water-spouting marble goldfish, one on its tail. "Greetings. Greetings," they called to me in their sweet little deadly voices. "Wishes for coins."

The sprites I'd encountered last time had had lime-green and raspberry-purple tresses. So the purple-haired one sitting on the goldfish's tail may or may not have been one of the two who had sent me over the cliff. But the other sprite, the one on the fish's head, had hair the pink of cotton candy, so she was definitely new.

Not that it mattered—not really. I didn't trust them in any case.

Gesturing toward the chest of treasures, I asked, "How many wishes will this get me?"

Cotton-Candy-Pink shook her head as though she were truly sorry. Yeah, right—like I believed that.

I pointed at the chest overflowing with—as they say in

fairy tales—a king's ransom, though I should think that how much ransom one was willing to pay would vary from king to king.

The sprite said, "Pretty." Then she shook her head again. "But not coins."

Her purple friend repeated, "Wishes for *coins*."

Coins, not goods.

Oh.

So much for my plan.

I stood there looking at the sprites with their oh-so-cute little faces, and their sweet smiles and lovely iridescent wings, and I considered my options. I had to work hard to keep from asking hammock-guy to take one of the dainty little creatures in each hand and hold them underwater.

"Wishes for coins," they reminded me with their musical giggles after a few moments, as though maybe I'd forgotten.

I knew from last time that they wouldn't volunteer any information. Maybe my plan didn't need to be scrapped entirely. Maybe we were just into Plan 1.1.

Picking up a diamond tiara, I said, "I want to sell this."

Was that a disgruntled look that passed between the two sprites?

But all they said was "Wishes for coins."

Wishes for coins. Wishes for coins. Had they been programmed by Rasmussem's lawyers?

I asked, "How many coins would it cost for me to make

a wish that this tiara would turn into its value-worth of coins?"

That was a definite pout on Purple's face.

Pink sounded as though she was speaking through her tiny clenched teeth. "Three coins for that wish."

I stuck my hand in my pocket, glad I had traded a butterfly for a coin each chance I'd had. I'd spent one on the misguided wish that had sent me tumbling over that cliff, which left me with . . . three coins.

Was it coincidence that the sprites asked for exactly as many as I had?

I asked, "How many coins would I get for wishing the tiara into coins?'

Purple stomped her tiny little heels into the water.

I had to ask Pink to repeat, since she grumbled her answer too softly for me to hear.

"One hundred fifty-seven," she mumbled. If looks could kill, I was guessing she'd be asking hammock-guy to hold *my* head underwater.

If they tricked me again, I'd be totally out of coins, but it wasn't like there was much else I could do with what I had.

I took a steadying breath, then threw the three coins into the water. "I wish," I said, being careful with my wording, because I knew they were just looking for a loophole, "for you to give me the one hundred fifty-seven gold coins that this tiara is worth." At the last second, I hurriedly added, "Right here," just in case they got it into their little heads to "give" me the money halfway around this mixed-up world. "Right now."

There was a sparkle of magic dust and a noise like the high notes of a xylophone, and—I have to admit—I braced myself to explode or turn into gold or get kicked out of the program—*something* wrong that I hadn't been clever enough to anticipate.

But all that happened was that the tiara I'd placed on the edge of the fountain disappeared, and in its place was a pile—a satisfyingly big pile—of gold coins.

The sprites glowered at me. I noticed that they did not offer their usual "Wishes for coins."

From the treasure chest, I picked up a hand-sized golden replica of the Victorian house. "How much," I asked, seeing the sprites squirm, "for a wish to turn *this* into its full value of gold?"

And so we went: all of Emily's gems, jewelry, golden artifacts, tableware, and knickknacks. How many times had my sister come to the sprites to get all this stuff? I wondered. And that brought up another thought: were the sprites nicer to her than they were to me? Because I knew I could never let my guard down. With each transaction, I chose my words oh-so-carefully, knowing that those treacherous little critters were looking for an opportunity to turn on me. Had they turned on Emily? Had they made her forget she had a family to go home to, regardless of how badly (I could only assume) Frank Lupiano had treated her?

By the time we were finished, the sprites had developed the habit of spitting every time they granted a wish. Which was just plain nasty, even if they were small and their spit sparkled.

There was no way the mound of coins would fit back into the chest. It wouldn't have fit into five chests. That kind of bulk was the reason credit cards were invented.

"How much," I asked, "for a small magical sack?" I indicated with my hands something change-purse-size, little enough to tie onto the sash of my dress. "The kind of magical sack that would hold everything I put in it but that would weigh no more than the sack itself?"

I left one chest's worth of coins out for hammock-guy to bring back to the pavilion, simply as a precaution, wealth just in case I had to start over again, dismantling Emily's Victorian house.

The sprites' hair was getting frizzled from their vexation at having to grant all my wishes.

"How much," I asked, "for me to have the power to turn into a dragon at will?"

Pink's hair actually sparked at that. And the answer was about half a treasure chest.

"That is just so attractive on you," I said to her. "Okay. Last wish—"

"Finally," Purple snapped.

I smiled at her. I smiled at both of them. "For now," I couldn't help but gloat.

They spat even before hearing my wish.

"How much would it cost for me to put you in the sack and take you with me?"

Changing into a dragon made me feel the way I imagine those Mentos candies felt when they were dropped into the bottles of Coke in that YouTube video: bubbly, fizzy, simultaneously dissolving and expansive, overflowing out of myself. While it was happening, it was out of control and scary. But it didn't hurt, and as soon as it was over—as soon as I realized I'd survived—I thought, *That was fun.*

I looked down at myself. I was much taller than the hedges that formed the maze. In fact, my sudden increase in size had uprooted a few of the bushes closest to me. My scales—I had scales!—were the shifting iridescent colors of soap bubbles. I had four legs, the front two short, a bit like *Tyrannosaurus rex* arms, and I also had wings. It didn't *feel* weird that I had an extra pair of appendages; it was only weird to think about. They looked too delicate to support my weight, but when I flapped them, I rose off the ground. I gave a couple more flaps, and I rose, sort of helicopter-like, out of the maze, over the garden, so that I could see the Victorian house and the pond with its swan-shaped gondola bobbing at its mooring. It was like looking at one of those

3-D miniature street scenes displayed at the Rochester Museum and Science Center—buildings and bridges and the river and the parks and the High Falls and the cemeteries—that show what the city looked like in the nineteenth century. Not that Rochester ever had gondolas. Or dragons, for that matter.

Pivoting my wings—dragon instincts must have come with the dragon body—I moved forward rather than straight up, and I circled the world I had explored already: House. Woods. Clearing with the tent. Clearing with the lute guy, where the unicorn had been.

But no Emily.

I was surprised to see that the sun was really low in the sky. Playing phone tag with Emily's so-called friends in the real world must have taken just about a whole day in this world.

That was not good, no matter how I looked at it.

I still held the magic sack in my talons—I hadn't tied it to the sash of my dress for fear that the bag would transform along with my clothing. And the clothing *had* transformed. Which was good—because a dragon in a thirty-sizes-too-small-Victorian-dress would have looked downright silly. Not to mention that dragonizing would have been hard on the seams. Now I shook the sack—which was only about the size of one talon—to get the attention of the sprites inside and called, "Where's Emily?"

When I couldn't hear a response, I shook the sack again.

Still nothing.

I put the sack up to my ear and only then could hear the tiny terrified shrieks of the sprites, and I realized I probably shouldn't have shaken the bag. "Oops, sorry," I said. If I had felt like Mentos mints, they probably felt like chicken drumsticks in a Shake 'n Bake bag.

"All right, all right, get over it," I told them.

Being a dragon, I was perfectly capable of flying while using my front paws. I loosened the drawstring, opening the bag.

Pink staggered out onto the stiff gathered edge of the sack, looking seasick-green and holding her hands over her ears. "Stop shouting!" she screamed at me.

Oops, I guess I'd been using my outside-dragon voice.

"Sorry," I repeated, whispering. "You and Purple all right?"

Pink indicated the bag behind her. "Inside. Barfing."

Ewww. I didn't care if it was sparkly like the spit had been; it was still barf. And all over my gold coins.

"Okay," I said. "No more shaking. Where's Emily?"

Pink just glowered at me.

"Where's Emily?" I repeated.

It took two more tries before I realized my wording was wrong.

"I wish for you to tell me where Emily is."

Grumbling, Pink said, "Wishes for coins."

"Go ahead," I told her. "Take one."

She didn't move.

Sighing, I reached into the sack and used the very tip of a talon to pull out a coin. Evidently, it was one of the ones Purple had been sick on: I could tell by the glittery pink coating. It was slightly tacky to the touch, but at least sprite spew didn't smell bad. It was sort of like talcum powder. "Here," I said.

Pink didn't move to take it. All she said was "Wishes for coins."

"What?" I demanded, frustrated that I couldn't tell what she wanted, even more frustrated because I *could* tell that she was enjoying this. "How many coins for telling me where Emily is?"

"The information costs one gold coin. Transporting you there costs five."

Remembering the last time they had transported me, I said, "Okay. I'll start with just the information."

She only smirked.

"I wish," I amended, "for you to tell me where Emily is."

Pink folded her arms over her chest and looked pleased with herself.

There were thousands of coins in my sack, I knew. What was different from the other times?

I sighed, and my dragon breath nearly singed a low-flying bird that had let us get too close. I angled my wings to change direction, and now Pink sighed, realizing I'd caught on.

Okay, if I needed the fountain for the wishes-for-coins magic to work, I'd bring *that* along with me, too.

The damn sprites weren't making things easy for me, but they weren't making things easy for themselves, either. I shook a whole dragon-fistful of coins out of the sack and into the water, announcing: "I wish for the fountain to go into the sack."

It disappeared from in front of me. From inside the bag, Purple gave a startled "Oomph!" But I knew the coins in there must have cushioned the weight, even if the fountain had landed directly on her, because she kicked the side of the bag and yelled out—in a tiny but very potty-mouth way—exactly what she thought of me.

"We hate you," Pink added as I flew up and into a big spiral over the house and grounds.

"Well, thanks for that free information. Where's Emily?"

Nothing.

"I wish for you to tell me."

Pink didn't spit, probably more from fear of the wind blowing the spittle back into her face than from fear of me. She mumbled, "Mountain castle."

In the distance, beyond the woods with the pavilion, I spotted some peaks. "Those mountains?"

She gave me a long *How dumb are you?* stare before I caught on and added, "Take another coin."

"Yes, those mountains," she answered.

"Don't you want to help Emily?" I asked, since everybody else here seemed to live to please my sister. I was hoping to get on Pink's good side. Did she have a good side? "All I'm trying to do is help Emily."

"Hate her worse than we hate you," Pink said venomously. "Cheaters, both of you. Too many coins. Too, too, too many coins."

"Oh," I said, not sure what to make of that. Then, not because I had a plan, but because I didn't want to look at her pouty face any more, I told her, "You can go back in the sack."

CHAPTER 13

Emily

THERE WAS A LAKE, and then beyond that, the mountains. No foothills: just woods, woods, woods (which sounds boring, except for the fact that: Hel-lo-o! I was *FLYING!*), then came the great turquoise sea, then mountains. The sky was dramatically pink and orange, and the sun appeared to be perched on the edge of the world when I finally arrived. I could see Emily's castle. Of course, it was on the summit with the best view.

I drifted in the air currents, feeling guilty about how much I'd enjoyed flying, wondering how I'd get Emily to come outside. And then I saw her, outdoors already. There was a balcony that went entirely around the highest parapet—the castle equivalent of the Victorian house's wraparound porch. She was leaning against a balustrade, watching the birds wheeling over the lake one last time before the sun set, and the dolphins cavorting in the sparkling water. There was even a rainbow—not that it had rained. A fine evening for enjoying the show nature—or rather, Rasmus-sem—was putting on.

Did my shadow cross over her? She looked up into the sky and raised her hand. For one exhilarating moment I thought she was acknowledging me, finally greeting me. Then I remembered I was a dragon, and she had no way of knowing that. She was simply shading her eyes, trying to cut out the glare of the sun behind me.

There were no reference points for her to gauge my distance or, therefore, guess at my size. If she saw me at all, she probably took me for a bird.

My dragon eyes—and the fact that I was *not* looking directly into the sun—let me see her clearly: the silver brocade dress that draped so elegantly, her hair ruffled by the breeze. She was the very picture of a queen. I aimed directly for her and dropped at full speed. Rushing . . . rushing . . . I saw in her eyes the moment she finally realized I was much too big, and moving far too quickly, to be another bird. Puzzlement turned to alarm. I'm not sure if alarm had time to turn into understanding; and by then I was within range.

Can I really do this?

I could. I had to.

I blasted my sister with my flaming dragon breath.

Dead on.

Not daring to flinch.

For one awful, awful moment I could see her silhouetted, the way you can sometimes make out a candle's wick through the surrounding flame. But then the fire got too big, too intense. By the time it dissipated and stopped licking at the metal railing, at the stone parapet, there was nothing left of Emily, not even ash. Still, I was breathing through my open mouth, not daring to inhale for fear of smelling charred meat. My sister. My sister, whom I had just burned alive.

The railing was drooping, the stones themselves were warped by the scorching, and if my dragon hide hadn't been so tough, the residual heat would have blistered my feet as I settled down on the balcony where she had been standing.

I had just killed Emily.

There would have been no pain, I told myself.

It's not for real, I told myself.

It's just a game, I told myself.

Like capturing the last piece in a game of checkers.

Myself was not convinced.

This didn't feel one bit like checkers.

Even if I *had* done it specifically to save her real life. To end the game and send her out of this fake world and back to Rasmussem.

I had been distraught when she'd had one of her game characters kill off another game character, and here I'd gone and killed her. Never mind that she'd done the same to me in exactly the same way, this simply felt wrong, wrong, wrong.

Had she felt this wretched when she'd killed me?

My body seemed to have developed a mind of its own. I was shaking, and something was boiling inside me, and for a moment I thought I was going to throw up. But it was a sob that bubbled out of me, a deep, racking sob. And then another, and another. I couldn't stop, couldn't catch my breath. My chest hurt. My heart hurt. The Rasmussem people would be ending the game any moment now—now that Emily had been forced back into reality—and I absolutely needed to regain control before I came to on the Rasmussem total immersion couch with everyone gawking at me. I was unwilling to make a show of myself in front of Ms. Bennett and Adam—plus, my mother would take one look at me and freak out.

I became aware that I was rocking back and forth on my knees, and that my knees hurt. They had sizzled a bit, from the intense heat, and they had little pieces of grit embedded in them. Knees. Human knees. Somewhere along the way, I had lost control of the wish to be a dragon and had reverted to being a girl. A girl who had just killed her sister.

And it was only then that I realized someone was standing over me.

"How sweet," Emily said in her snarkiest tone, the one she normally used for mocking people on TV, not family. "You killed me, but you're sad about it. Oh, well! I guess that makes everything all right."

Emily?

Okay, I'm back at Rasmussem after all, I thought. I hadn't even felt the transition. I braced myself for embarrassment.

Except I wasn't back on the total immersion couch. I was still on the castle parapet.

So how could Emily be there?

But *there* she indeed was, as big as life: glaring at me, tapping her gemstone-sandaled foot, even.

I rubbed my snot and tears off on my already-filthy sleeve. My throat hurt, my head hurt. But my heart felt just a little bit better.

"Emily," I managed to gasp between the sobs that still wouldn't stop, "I'm sorry I tried to kill you. I'm glad you got away." That was true *despite* my realization that this was a major setback.

How had she gotten away?

My mind refused to focus on the thought that she couldn't have—because she obviously had.

That wasn't important now. What was important was explaining to her why I had done what I'd done.

She spoke before I could get my mouth to work. "That getting-away part?" she said. "Not so much. You *did* kill me. But I came back."

I was glad to see her. I guess. Not quite as glad as I'd have been if we were both back at Rasmussem, but it was a relief, no matter how I looked at it, that I hadn't done a thorough job of killing my sister.

I gulped in enough air to ask, "What do you mean you came back?" I tried to make sense out of her not being dead, of my having gone through all that—the decision, the doing, the watching—of having killed her, all for nothing. "You returned to Rasmussem and they . . . ?" Except they wouldn't have. They wouldn't send her here to fetch me. *I* wanted out of this inane game; *she* was the one who was resisting . . .

But she was shaking her head. "Not to Rasmussem," she explained. "I adjusted the code so that if I got killed, I would just restart from the same place."

Wonderful. Everything I'd been through was meaningless.

And I knew I could never do it again.

I swatted away one of a pair of sparkly monarch butterflies that were trying to alight on our arms.

"I can't believe," Emily snarled at me, "that you actually killed me."

All right, this was just getting to be too much. "Oh," I said. "So you're going to insist on taking that personally?"

She put her hands on her hips. "Well, *yeah.*"

"Excuse me, but you killed me first."

"Oh, sure," Emily countered. "Put the blame on me."

"Nice," I snarled right back at her. "Who's the one who's been trying all along to get rid of me, trying to lose yourself in this, the world's most . . ." I couldn't think of a word to encapsulate all that I felt about this game. ". . . pink . . . and . . . and . . . pointless . . . and . . ."

"Then go home if you don't like it," Emily snapped. "I never invited you to join me. I don't want you here."

Much as I knew that already, it hurt to be told. "Yeah, and you've made that plenty clear."

"So what are you waiting for? Go."

"Oh, yeah?" I shot back at her, realizing even as I said it that we had degenerated to the level of feuding first-graders.

Emily lowered to the occasion. "Yeah."

She's trying to make me mad, I realized. She wanted to goad me into leaving. And that realization quenched my anger. I took a calming breath and told her, "Not without you."

Which defused her. Either that or she realized how ridiculous we sounded. Emily sighed. She said what she'd been saying all along, but this time she sounded more tired than annoyed. "Go back, Grace. I'm not coming home. Just leave me. This is all for the best. Really."

"No," I said. "Whatever's happened back home, it can be fixed."

Emily swerved back into annoyed. "You don't know anything about it."

"We talked to Danielle," I told her. "And Frank."

Emily narrowed her eyes. "And what did they say?"

I weighed my options. I didn't know enough to be able to bluff, so I went in the opposite direction. "They have no idea what's wrong."

"The liars!" Emily shouted. Now she sat down next to me, and the next thing I knew she began to cry. "The liars," she repeated. "That is just so damn frustrating."

Well, that was unexpected. "Tell me," I said.

And she finally did.

"Danielle and I planned . . . We've been planning just about all our lives . . . to go to school together. And RIT was perfect for both of us: me to study total immersion technology, her to learn to be a commercial textile artist. Then we took our college entrance exams."

SATs. I was only in ninth grade, two more years to go before I'd take them, but our teachers were already warning us that those could mean more than whatever marks we've gotten in our classes. But only, it seemed, in a negative way. Good scores couldn't counteract mediocre grades, but bad scores could sink our hopes of getting into a specific college.

Emily was saying, "And Danielle . . . Danielle's scores were middle-of-the-road. Not high enough for RIT. And it isn't because Danielle is a dummy. Well, she is . . . because she didn't take the PSATs or the sample tests to practice, and she was out partying the night before, and she came dragging in that morning energized by Diet Coke and Hershey's Kisses. I told her she could take the exam again, but she kept saying she just doesn't test well because she gets all nervous. That she knew she could do the work, but the SAT was the end for her."

"Okay," I said, remembering the whole plan where she could go to community college for one semester. "I know this."

"No, you don't. Because what happened was she said, 'You're so good with computers, and the SATs are all computerized.' "

It took a moment for that to sink in, the words spoken to Emily. My sister, the computer genius. "She asked you to change her SAT scores?" What kind of friend would ask someone to cheat like that for her? Well, okay, a desperate friend. "So she's mad because you wouldn't do it?"

Emily chewed on her lip.

"You *did* do it?" I squeaked. "You could do that?" Of course. I'd forgotten for a moment who I was talking to: the only person in the history of Western civilization— or at least at Neil Armstrong High—who thrived on trigonometry. "But then," I asked, "why . . . I mean . . . what happened?"

"First," Emily said, "I did it. I bumped her scores up. And then . . . *then* she told Frank. And Frank wanted his scores bumped, too, so that he could get a scholarship. 'Boston's accepted me, Emily,' he said, 'but my parents can't afford the tuition. If my scores were just a little bit higher, I'd be eligible for financial aid.' "

I could just picture the weasel putting her on the spot. "Did you do it?" I asked.

"At first I said no, and he said, 'You'll do it for your *girl-*

friend, but not for your *boyfriend?*" So finally, I gave in. And the next thing I knew, Frank was telling *his* friends—"

"Ungrateful jerk," I interrupted.

She continued, "And other people were coming to me, telling me they couldn't get into the college of their dreams. Crying. Begging for help."

I was glad I wasn't smart enough that I'd ever have to face a moral dilemma like whether to help a friend cheat. The only kind of cheating my friends and I were likely to get caught up in involved dieting.

Emily said, "And I couldn't help all of them. I couldn't fiddle with all their scores. I mean, some of them had never gotten above a C+ their entire academic life. How would anyone believe they'd ever ace their SATs? So I had to say no."

Surely her friends had to understand.

But apparently not.

Emily was saying, "And Frank said he was embarrassed in front of our friends, even though he got his stupid scholarship—but Danielle ended up not making the cut anyway. And she said it was all my fault for not making her marks high enough. She asked why I hadn't given her the same exact marks I'd gotten, so that we'd have been sure to be accepted or turned down together. She said I was just jealous, that I wanted to make sure everyone knew *I* was the smart one. But that wasn't it. I was only trying not to be obvious about it. My marks in high school had always been higher than hers, so the guidance counselors would have been suspicious if I'd given her exactly the same marks."

Now it was Emily's turn to wipe her nose on her sleeve.

"In the end, my classmates weren't talking to me anymore, and if any of them ever rats me out, the people at RIT will suspect that I fudged my own marks, too, and I'll get tossed out. If not tossed into jail. I thought they were my friends, Grace."

She hunched over and closed her eyes.

She had been betrayed by her friends, and I could only imagine how that felt. "I didn't know," I said, only to say something to fill in the silence that sat so heavily around us. "I always felt . . ." I didn't finish the thought. *I always felt you were the blessed one. You had everything. The looks. The smarts. ALL the friends. The boys. The social life I wished for . . .*

As though she could read my mind, Emily looked up at me and said, "So now you know the truth, how stupid and empty my life really is."

Our parents would be disappointed, and she was right: the school would probably bounce her out on her ear, even if they believed her scores, for helping other people cheat.

"But it's not worth dying over," I told her.

"It's not like dying," she said. "It's like fading away."

"It's dying," I insisted. "And, sure, your so-called friends might feel guilty and be sorry . . ." Obviously, this was part of it: Everyone who has ever been wronged thinks, *If I were dead, THEN they'd be sorry . . .* "But, Emily," I continued, "think what it will do to Mom and Dad. Think what it'll do to me. They sent me in to rescue you, Emily. I've never been as smart as you, but if I fail at this . . ." My throat closed up again.

"Oh, Grace," Emily said, "it's not you. You're the best little sister anyone ever had. You're making this harder than it needs to be. You've always been brave and resourceful and you're good at figuring out common-sense things. You'd never have gotten yourself into this situation."

I didn't believe those words described me, but they were nice to hear. They were the first kind words Emily had spoken to me since I'd arrived. Here, *here* was the big sister I knew and loved, who had always looked out for me.

I said, "Tell Mom and Dad everything. They'll get over a bit of cheating to try to help friends much more easily than they'll get over my not being able to save you."

Emily said, slowly and emphatically, as though speaking to a stubborn preschooler, "It's not about you, Grace." She shook her head. "Back at Neil Armstrong, I thought I had all these great friends, but they only wanted to use me. Now I'm in college, and they don't even bother to pretend, because I'm not worth the effort."

"Now you're just feeling sorry for yourself," I told her.

She shrugged.

I countered with the only thing I had left. "You're my sister," I said. "And I love you."

Emily rested her hand on my cheek, another first in

this miserable game, a warm and gentle gesture that was *just* like what I would have expected from her in the past. "I love you, too," she told me, "but I've messed things up big-time. *Here*, too. I don't even like it here anymore."

"No kidding," I said. "This game should come with a warning label: might induce diabetes, hyperactivity, and tooth decay."

She gave a sad smile.

"Emily," I said, "come home. Please. Don't make me become the one who let you die." And once more, tears started running down my cheeks.

She closed her eyes again, maybe so she wouldn't have to look at me crying. It wasn't acting on my part; I didn't think it out, as in *Ooo, I'll get louder so she can't ignore me—* but I started sobbing again, huge, wheezing sobs.

"Grace," Emily murmured.

I smacked her hand away from my face, not willing to take any comfort from her except for the comfort of her coming with me. "You can say it's not about me, but it's not *only* about you. Danielle and Frank and the rest of them will get over feeling bad. Mom and Dad and I won't."

"You will," Emily reassured me.

"I should never have let them talk me into coming," I said. "I should have known I'd fail." Okay, that was acting. A bit. At the moment I said it.

But as soon as the words were out of my mouth, I realized they were true. This was just too big a job for me.

Emily's shoulders slumped, and she looked close to crying again, too. "I'm sorry," she said. "I'm sorry, I'm sorry, I'm sorry. The last thing I wanted to do was hurt you. I wanted to protect you. But if I go back, what then? What will happen to me?"

I had to admit it. "I don't know. It can't be any worse than this."

Emily finally agreed with something I said. "And I couldn't feel any worse. Please don't cry like that. I'm sorry I've been so mean to you. I just wanted you to go back home."

Mean? Mean was eating all the chocolate Easter eggs and leaving the stale Peeps. *Mean* was making fun of a bad hairstyle. *Mean* was letting someone else take the blame after *you* tracked mud onto the clean floor. *Mean* didn't begin to cover what Emily had put me through.

But she was rocking me, making gentle comforting noises as though I were once again the six-year-old who'd fallen off our backyard swing trying to fly too high. "Everything will be okay."

And then, finally—finally—she said the magic words that would end my ordeal: "End game. Bring me back to Rasmussem."

My voice came out as a whisper. "Thank you, Emily." I had to try twice before I, too, could manage to speak the Rasmussem formula out loud: "End game. Bring me back to

Rasmussem." Precise wording, so it can't be spoken accidentally. Was it ever spoken so much from the heart?

Of course, with time moving differently in the game, we didn't bounce back like yo-yos at the end of a string, but it would be soon now.

Exhausted from all our tears, we leaned against each other and counted stars in the now-dark sky until we fell asleep in each other's arms.

We woke up, stiff and sore and sooty, when the sun peeked up over the horizon.

And we were still in the game.

CHAPTER 14

I Guess That Would Be Another *Oops!*

A FTER ALL THAT.

Still in the Land of the Golden Butterflies, still on the tower balcony of Emily's mountain castle overlooking the sparkly lake.

There were even a couple of those damn butterflies fluttering around our heads, as though everything were lovely and normal, as though—after all we'd been through—we'd still be in the mood to transform them into coins for just another day of good, clean, wholesome fun.

"What happened?" I asked, suspecting—I admit it—Emily had somehow tricked me. But even as the words were coming out of my mouth, I knew that couldn't be it: if Emily had only been pretending to agree to return home in order to get rid of me, wouldn't I have found myself back there without her?

"That . . ." Emily said, ". . . that shouldn't have happened." Her worried expression did even more than my reasoning had to convince me that she was just as surprised and confused and concerned as I was. "We should be back home." I don't know if something of my initial mistrust showed in my face or voice, but Emily added, "Truly, Grace."

"Okay," I said, trying to bury with words the unease that was gnawing at my stomach. This was supposed to be over. We were supposed to be back in the real world. We were supposed to be safe. Both of us. "Well, maybe we just need to say it again. Maybe we didn't say it loudly enough, or clearly enough. 'Cause . . . you know . . . we were crying and all . . . Maybe."

"It can't hurt to try," Emily said. But she was just being the comforting big sister. Her face was saying: *It can't help, either.*

Still wary—see what being abandoned in a maze, tossed out of a royal ball, and flame-roasted by a dragon will do to a girl?—I waited for Emily to speak first. She did. "End game. Bring me back to Rasmussem," she said. Again.

And I repeated it. Again. "End game. Bring me back to Rasmussem."

We waited. Again.

While doing all that waiting, I noticed—I can be *such* an observant soul!—that Emily had a leopard-print blanket around her. And—oh, yeah!—so did I. They were both a really soft, plush fake fur: hers, regular leopard; mine, pink leopard—which was what led me to suspect the fur was fake, although in this place, maybe not. Maybe the pink leopards periodically shed their fur in order to play with their best friends, the lake dolphins.

Whatever the origins of the blankets, someone must have been worried about us getting cold. I looked beyond Emily, through the open French doors that led inside, into the tower part of the castle. I could see a huge, elegant Renaissance-style bedroom, round because of the curved walls of the tower, all crystal and gilded surfaces. A couple of her guys—her strong, good-looking, silent servant guys—were hovering inside, right by the door, where they could see us. One was arranging and rearranging and *re*-rearranging flowers in a vase. The other had a feather duster, and he was going over the table that held the vase as though the wood were really thousand-year-old paper and the slightest pressure would cause it to collapse. Both of them being totally obvious about keeping an eye on us.

"Completely harmless," Emily assured me.

But they were, apparently, able to act on their own, to note that the temperature had gone down with the setting of the sun, and to fetch coverings for us.

Which was kind.

But couldn't they have, just as easily, chosen *not* to be kind?

We were stuck here with game characters who had free

will. Uneasily, I let the blanket they had given me slip off my shoulders. Still, being my mother's daughter, I couldn't just leave it there in a heap on the parapet, and so I folded it. Only then—finally—did I notice something else.

There was no sack, no gold-coin-and-sprite-and-wishing-fountain sack, anywhere on the balcony.

I took Emily's blanket from her and held it up. Shook it, even, in case the sack had gotten caught in its folds while the blanket had been dragging along the floor.

"What?" Emily asked.

I tried to think back to yesterday, to approaching the castle, to seeing Emily . . . I forced myself to stay with the memories, right through killing her, then to landing on the super-heated stones of the parapet.

I *had* been holding the sack in my dragon talons; I knew I had.

"What?" Emily repeated.

"I had a sack of gold," I told her.

"Not chief among our worries." She began pacing, knowing as well as I did that Rasmussem was not going to be pulling us back.

I persisted. "But there were sprites in it. And their magic fountain."

She raised her eyebrows at me. "Interesting. But *important* because . . . ?"

"We could wish to go back," I said.

She gave me much the same look as when I'd suggested we should simply try repeating our desire to go home.

"And," I said, "*and* it's one more thing gone wrong that shouldn't have."

That, I could see, struck her as a much more meaningful argument. The accumulation of things gone wrong was getting oppressive.

Emily bent over and walked back and forth, scrutinizing the stone floor. Suddenly, she crouched down and ran her fingers over the surface. "Look," she told me.

I got down next to her and saw—in the residue of soot my dragon flame had left—a smudge. "What is it?"

"What's it look like?"

I hate it when people go into teacher mode like that. "If I knew, I wouldn't have asked."

"Well, this part over here looks to me," Emily said, "like teeny tiny footprints. And here, where the footprints are obliterated, I think something was dragged."

I finished for her: "Something like a sprite-powered sack full of gold?"

The smudges continued across the stone balcony floor until they passed through the French doors and into the bedroom. There, the floor was white and gold tiles. And clean. Impeccably clean. I put my hands on my hips and glared at the servant with the feather duster, who pretended not to notice me as he ran his duster over the other servant's shoulders.

"You really think this is important?" Emily asked me.

"Yeah," I said. "For some reason, the sprites have taken an intense dislike to the two of us."

"No," Emily said. "They love me."

"Not as much as you might think," I told her. "I need to find them, and, thanks to your very efficient servants, the trail ends here."

"It only ends to human eyes," she told me, "and noses."

In the moment I took to try to figure that out, Emily transformed into a bloodhound.

Oh, I realized, *she must have wished for the ability to transform into WHATEVER at will.* I had specifically asked for dragon shaping. I didn't need to experiment: I knew the sprites hadn't extended my wish to fit with my sister's.

Bloodhound Emily put her nose to the floor and started sniffing.

I followed, wishing I'd asked the sprites for a comfortable pair of sneakers while I'd had the chance. Or that I'd asked Emily to wait a sec so I could rummage through her closet for a pair of *her* shoes, because I'd been off balance since losing that one right before I went over the cliff. But now there was no time—for regrets or for rummaging. I had to move fast or risk losing her as she tracked the sprites through that tower bedroom, down a long spiral flight of stairs that brought us out of the tower and into the castle proper, through a big ballroom, down a flight of regular stairs, down a hallway, through an entry hall, outdoors, down four marble steps, through a courtyard, beyond the castle wall, and down a path that led through an Alpine meadow. Since the path was dirt, I could pick up the trail here myself. Yeah, and the telltale little cloud of dust moving down the path away from us was another strong clue.

Emily sat on her haunches and bayed, which I guess showed that just as I'd gotten dragon instincts when I turned into a dragon, bloodhound instincts automatically came with her new shape. But now that our quarry was in sight, she switched out of her doggy form back to being Emily.

We ran up to the dust cloud, which was being thrown up into the air by the scurrying of two pairs of sprite feet moving at top sprite speed. Strictly speaking, Pink and Purple were still inside the bag. They had their scrawny arms up over their heads, holding on to the open neck of the sack as though it were a huge hoodie for two, while the body of the sack dragged and bounced and jingled and gurgled behind them.

I worked it out from a legalistic point of view, since Pink and Purple gave every appearance of being tiny lawyers-in-training. Okay, I had wished for—and paid for—the two of them to go into the sack, along with the gold and the wishing fountain. So they couldn't just get up and magically spirit (or would that be *sprite*?) themselves out of there. Even flying home—and that was assuming their tiny wings would be able to hold out that distance—put them on shaky ground, legally speaking. But, treacherous little fiends that they were, they apparently didn't think it against the rules of our agreement to walk home so long as they were still at least 50 percent inside the sack.

I stepped around them and stood in their way. "Excuse me," I said.

Pink gave a groan of disgust. "Told you to walk faster," she snapped at Purple.

Emily crouched down in front of them. "Hello, little sprites," she said as though addressing adorable miniature two-year-olds.

Pink kicked Emily on the ankle. "Hate you," she said. "Hate you, hate you, hate you."

Purple almost knocked Pink down in her attempt to also get a kick in, all the while still holding on to the sack. "Hate you, too," she spat at Emily.

"Yeah, right," I said to Emily, "I'm really feeling the love here."

"I don't understand this," Emily said, half to me, half to them.

Pink pretended Emily had a language problem and made like a thesaurus: "Hate: despise, detest, hold in contempt, have an abhorrence for, loathe, feel revulsion toward, suffer an aversion to, dislike"—and here she overenunciated every syllable while at the same time relishing every instant of hate-spew—"ex-*treme*-ly."

"But why?" Emily asked. "What have I done?"

Purple screamed and pulled her own hair in frustration. Which, of course, meant she let go of her section of the sack edge, so the fabric all but engulfed the two little malignancies.

Emily plucked the trailing sack up to be able to see and hear them better.

"Keep changing the rules!" Pink shouted at her. "Cheater! Make more butterflies, make more flowers, make more cash prizes at the arcade!"

"There's an arcade?" I asked.

"Too many coins!" Purple screamed.

"Too many wishes!" Pink yelled.

In unison the two of them shrieked: "Too easy! Dirty, dirty cheater!"

"No, really," I said, "don't hold back. Tell us how you feel."

"Oh," Emily said.

The crack in her voice made me turn away from the sprites to my sister. She looked ready to cry.

Over the sprites?

But then it came to me: over the betrayal. First her friends turned on her, then this world she had tried to form into a safe refuge did the same.

And here I was, taking sarcastic potshots at her and the sprites indiscriminately.

Before I could apologize to her, she apologized to the sprites. "I'm sorry," Emily said.

"Not," Pink grumbled.

"Not sorry," Purple agreed.

"But I am," Emily insisted.

I could see where she was going. The servants could take action on their own, so what would happen if the sprites could, too? If the sprites of this world could take offense at us, they might well be behind what was going wrong here, why we couldn't go back. So, for good measure, I indicated that I was contrite also. "Me too."

The sprites ignored me. Still speaking to Emily, Pink said in a pouty voice, "If you're sorry"—and here she shook the sack she was still holding up over her head—"if you're truly sorry, reverse this stupid spell your stupid cheater sister put on us."

"Hey," I protested. Okay, I could understand they were peeved with us, but *stupid? Stupid cheater? Me?*

Purple shook her head as though to show she'd *known* we couldn't be trusted. "Not sorry," she said to her sister sprite in an I-told-you-so tone. "Not really."

"Of course I am," Emily protested. And to prove her good intentions, she said, "I wish for you to be released from the spell Grace put on you."

As soon as she said it, I caught on. Two seconds too late. "No!" I shouted.

It was the one wish they granted for free. Tossing the sack up in the air away from them, the two sprites sneered at us. "Goodbye, losers!" they cackled. Sprites, gold, wishing fountain, and sack disappeared.

"Oops," Emily said.

CHAPTER 15

Dragon Flight

W ELL, that's a kick in the pants," I said, looking at the place where the sprites no longer were, as though if I spoke in an it's-no-big-deal tone, then this latest setback would turn out to be no more than a minor inconvenience. "Can you call them back?"

"How?" Emily snapped, sounding testy, sounding as though *I* were responsible for the sprites' bad disposition. "You mean, like, 'Yoohoo! Sprites! Please come back! Oh! And if you can't do that, then could you kindly send us home to Rasmussem!' Something like that?"

So much for elevating the morale here. "Hey!" I said, putting my hands on my hips.

"What?" She got right up into my face.

"This is not my fault."

"No, it isn't," she snarled. "You're absolutely right: it's all my fault. Every stinking bit of it."

"That isn't what I meant."

"But it's what you're thinking," Emily said. She looked

around, and I could tell she was searching for something to throw, or to break—some destructive action she could perform to express her extreme frustration. But there was nothing handy, and all she could do was kick at the recently sprite-vacated spot. "Every single damn thing I do turns out wrong. It was fine for me to just lose myself in the game and never come back, but now you're stuck here, too."

Her regret cooled down my anger. "I'm not blaming you," I said. "I was just asking if you had some sort of sprite-summoning spell."

"No." She practically spat out the word, *her* temper still at full blaze. "No, I was not clever enough to think of that. Just like I was not clever enough to come up with some better solution to my real-life problems than to do something that would hurt Mom and Dad and now endanger you. I am leaving behind a legacy of destruction that will have everyone hating me when I'm gone."

The reminder that we were both in very real physical danger was not doing anything to clarify my thinking. Still, sniping at each other would accomplish nothing.

"All right," I said, "so what do you want to do? Fight with me? Break things? Give up? And just sit here waiting to die, grumbling about how unfair it is?"

"No," she admitted sulkily.

"Okay," I said, "if we can't force the sprites to come back here, then we'll have to go to them wherever they are. Which I assume would be back in the center of the maze?"

Emily shrugged.

"Is that where you first found them?"

She gave a nod that was hardly more enthusiastic than the shrug.

Since she wasn't being much help at all, I finished, "And I'm assuming there's no instant teleportation spell or device . . ."

She shook her head.

". . . so the fastest way to get there would be the way I came: flying in our dragon forms?"

Emily summoned the energy to mutter, "I guess."

"Okay," I said. "So what are we waiting for?"

Emily raised her arms, and in the blink of an eye she was a bronze dragon. She was huge, her head far longer than I was tall. And she was beautiful. As well as terrible. Her wings flapped once, twice, slow, majestic moves that displaced enough air that the resulting wind almost knocked me over. But then she was rising: over my head, then tree-level, then bird-level. She circled, waiting for me.

"I wish to be a dragon," I said, though I hadn't needed to say it out loud the first time, nor had Emily spoken any words.

I held my arms out.

I flapped them.

I bunny-hopped to break contact between my feet and the ground.

How had I done it last time?

I had simply wished it, and it happened.

So what was wrong this time?

Knowing the sprites' tendency toward treachery, I had been very careful with what I'd asked for, not wanting my metamorphosis into a dragon to be a one-shot deal, just in case, nor wanting it to be irreversible—also just in case. I had worked out the wording in my head beforehand, so I remembered exactly what I had wished for and paid for: I had asked for the power to turn into a dragon at will.

Okay, I thought, *I'm willing it now.*

Emily glided back down to earth and hovered before me in all her dragon splendor. "What's the delay?" she asked, her voice her own, despite her dragon body.

"You reversed my spell," I said. "Apparently, those demon-spawned sprites took that to mean *all* my spells."

Emily sighed, the warm air of her breath like a mega-hair dryer on my entire body. She settled to the ground. "I'll carry you," she said, reaching a dragon claw toward me.

"No way!" I scrambled backward, remembering how hard I'd had to clutch the sack to maintain a firm hold. "Lose your concentration while you're flying, and if you didn't puncture me with your talons or squeeze the life out of me with your grip, you'd drop me."

Emily studied her claw. "Dragons should come with opposable thumbs," she mused.

"Yeah," I said, "take it up with Rasmussem's design department. How about if I climb onto your back and ride you?"

Uh-huh. Easier said than done. Even when she lay flat on the ground, I would have had to climb like three times my height. And her scales were hard and slippery. She picked me up—very careful not to puncture, squeeze, or drop—but her arms weren't long enough to go around to her back: another definite design flaw.

"All right," Emily said. "We'll return to my castle. I'll wait under one of the tower windows, and you can go up there and jump out on my back."

"Jump out a window onto your back?" I repeated.

"Yes," she said.

"And count on not killing myself in the process?"

"What do you mean?"

"I mean," I explained, "what if I miss?"

Emily snorted, singeing my eyebrows. "I'm a pretty large target to miss."

"Yeah," I said, "but I could slide right off you and hit the ground, and there wouldn't be any way for you to catch me." I tucked my elbows in close to my body and waggled my shortened arms helplessly, dragonlike.

"Well, if you die . . ." she started. But she didn't finish. The truth was, we didn't know what would happen if I died in the game world. The previous times, I had returned to Rasmussem, but things had changed. And we didn't know how much. We couldn't count on anything happening now the way we thought it should. I remembered the pain I had inflicted on myself with that rock that had bounced off the ballroom window. What if, now, I couldn't die in the game, but could still feel the pain of injuries, even deadly injuries?

"All right, all right," Emily said impatiently—but the fact that she said it at all showed she was reasoning along the same lines I was. "No diving out of windows." She looked at me as though evaluating. "I wonder," she said, "if I could pick you up in my mouth by taking hold of your head, very gently, using just my lips . . ." She tried curling her dragon lips over her dragon teeth. ". . . I could kind of swing you around . . ." She angled her massive head over her shoulder to see how far back she could reach.

I, of course, had lost it the moment she'd said she'd take my head in her mouth. I think I finally got through to her the fifteenth or sixteenth time I chanted *no*.

"All right, then, Grace," she said, "*your* turn to make a suggestion *I* can poke holes in."

Since I wasn't able to get rid of the mental image of her dragon teeth making Swiss cheese of my skull, that was unfortunate phraseology on her part.

"How about," I suggested, "if you lie down again, and you don't tuck your front arms under you, but stretch one of them out, sort of like a ramp for me to use?"

Scornfully, Emily muttered, "A handicapped-accessible dragon," but did as I suggested.

I scrambled my way up talon, wrist, forearm, elbow, before I saw there was just too much back muscle for me to be able to climb farther.

"Can't do it," I told her. "May I try it on your wing?" Sort of the way a kite is made with paper stretched over a wooden frame, the dragon's wing was leather stretched over bone. Being careful to put my weight only on the edge of the wing, I hauled myself up onto my sister's back. It was no harder than, for example, climbing up that stupid rope they have in obstacle courses—which, by the way, I've never been able to do.

But, eventually, I made it. I even found a relatively flat spot between her wings to sit. Well, actually, I was more lying belly-down, since that seemed more secure. Except, of course, that her scales were already scratchy on my face—dermabrasion for the fantasy set. "Okay," I said, summoning all my bravery and my optimism, "this might work."

Then she flapped her wings, and that changed everything. "Down," I screamed. "Down, down, down!"

"Just hold on," Emily said.

"To what?" I yelped.

She rose higher and higher into the air.

"No! Stop! Let me get off!" But meanwhile, I finagled my fingers under one of her scales to have something to hold on to, all the while wondering how likely it was that I'd accidentally pluck out the scale.

"See, you're fine," Emily said.

"No wonder the sprites hate you," I told her.

Emily didn't answer, and I realized it had been a cheap shot. What I should be doing was working hard to raise her spirits so she wasn't so depressed. But I mean, come on!

As wonderful as flying in my dragon shape had been, flying *on* a dragon was the exact opposite. Even going beyond the sheer terror of I'm-going-to-fall-and-plummet-something-like-a-gazillion-feet-to-the-ground-and-go-splat!-and-probably-still-not-have-the-luxury-of-being-dead-despite-the-fact-that-I'll-be-feeling-every-shattered-bone-and-ruptured-organ, it was not comfortable riding on the dragon's back, and every wing flap tipped me forward, backward, and sideways. Emily was flying no higher and no faster than I'd been, but my stomach was lurching. Yet I knew if I started throwing up, I'd be sure to fall off. I tried closing my eyes, thinking that might cut down on the dizziness, but it added to the out-of-control feeling. Plus, I kept picturing the inhabitants of the Land of the Golden Butterflies going, "Ick! It's raining vomit!" which made me even queasier. I figured I would be likelier to maintain my balance and stay on the dragon, plus keep my stomach contents actually inside my stomach, if I could see what was happening.

I won't say it got easier with time, as my hands and arms ached from holding on to the scale so tightly, and the panic didn't exactly fade, but a certain numbness set in.

And time did pass.

A lot of it.

And eventually, I realized that Emily was gliding downward.

"Are we there?" I asked.

It didn't look like we were there.

All I could see was forest, no Victorian house on the edge of a lake.

"No," Emily said. "I just need a rest."

There was a river cutting through the forest where Emily found a section of bank with a large, level sandy spot and coasted in.

"Do you know where you're going?" I asked. "Are we lost? I didn't need a rest stop when I was flying."

"You weren't carrying you," Emily said. She transformed back to herself just as I shifted my position to sitting up, and for one totally weird moment I was sitting on her back while she was standing up—and then I slid down and hit the ground, butt first.

"Besides," Emily added, sounding defensive, "I haven't eaten since lunch with the gypsies yesterday."

"Ooo, lunch with the gypsies," I mimicked, since the only food that had passed my lips in this game had been that single cinnamon cookie when I'd first arrived. I *was* hungry, I realized.

"I'm going to take a nap," Emily said. "Just a few minutes. Maybe you can make yourself useful and find something to eat."

"Find something?" I echoed. "Like what? Lake dolphins? Unicorns? What *does* one eat here?"

"All the fruits are edible," Emily said. "If there are gypsies nearby, they always have stuff like hot dogs, and taco salads, and macaroni and cheese."

Ah! The traditional foods.

She lay down right where she was, making no attempt to smooth the sand or form it into a hollow or anything more comfortable, and curled herself up small. "Can you look, please, Grace? I really need to sleep. Then we can eat whatever you've found and be back at the house by mid-afternoon."

"Okay," I said. "I guess." I was hungry and tired, too. But had carrying me been *that* hard for Emily, or was this a symptom of her having been in the game too long? Was her real-life body beginning to weaken? And if so, would virtual food and rest help?

No chance to ask Emily her thoughts, as she was asleep already.

There shouldn't be anything here dangerous enough that Emily would need me to stand guard, I thought. *This is just a little kids' game.*

Yeah, right. There were a lot of *shouldn't*s in this game.

I found a blackberry bush close enough that I could pick while still keeping Emily in sight. It was hard not to eat more than half, but I was just hungry, not in danger of fading—at least not yet.

When my fingers were purple and sticky, not to mention cramped from berry picking, I sat down in a grassy patch and waited for my sister to wake up.

I hadn't caught any of the golden butterflies the previous day when I'd had a sack full of gold coins, and I certainly hadn't been in the mood earlier while holding on to Emily's dragon scales for dear life. But now, while I waited, I caught half a dozen butterflies and turned them into coins. By counting "One Mississippi, two Mississippi . . ." I estimated that they came every five minutes or so, in pairs, evidently one for each of us. But after a while, that got so boring, I fell asleep despite my best intentions.

I awoke to find that what was left of the morning had turned to afternoon, and the berries I'd saved for Emily were beginning to dry out and look old, and finally I gave her a nudge. Then another. "Emily!" I called, shaking her shoulder, convinced I wouldn't be able to rouse her.

Her eyes fluttered open. "Grace," she said, "really, please just give me five minutes."

"You've slept something like three hours already."

"No," she mumbled, closing her eyes again, and settling back into her fetal position.

I had newfound sympathy for what our mother went through, trying to get us up for school.

"Emily," I said, shaking her harder, "you need to wake up now."

"All right, all right," she grumbled, but she made no move.

I grabbed her by the shoulders and forced her up to a sitting position. "Now," I said sternly.

She sighed and finally opened her eyes. "All right," she said, sounding a bit more convincing this time. "All right." She yawned and stretched. "Did you get something to eat?"

I nodded toward the pile of berries, which looked pretty paltry considering how sore my fingers had gotten. "And," I pointed out, "another couple hours and we'll be back at the house. We can confront the sprites, and if they can't send us back home right away, we can eat in your kitchen."

Emily, busy snarfing the berries down by the handful rather than savoring them one by one, didn't sound too enthusiastic about my plan. But she said, "All right."

"And," I said, "I think I figured a way how to get on your back more easily."

"Okay . . ." she said warily.

"You can change into any animal, right?"

She nodded.

"Turn yourself into a Saint Bernard."

"That'll be useful," she scoffed. "You *do* know I won't

come with one of those little barrels of brandy or whatever it is that those rescue dogs in the Alps have?"

"No, that's okay. What I'm thinking is that you can turn into a dragon gradually . . . in different steps . . . getting bigger and bigger."

Emily still looked skeptical, but that's what we did. She turned into a big dog, and I straddled her, not putting my weight on her back until she morphed into a pony; then she became a full-sized horse; then an elephant; then she dragonized herself. There's a significant difference between an elephant and a dragon, but at least I was in position.

The flying was no more pleasant on this leg of the journey, and Emily tired out after a much shorter time. She wanted to stop again ("Just for a little bit, Grace"), but I begged and cajoled, and finally we were flying over the part of the forest I'd seen already, and that gave her the extra impetus she needed.

By then, Emily was trembling with exhaustion, and her scales had lost much of their luster. We landed in the maze, not a graceful touchdown at all this time, and we flattened a whole wall of bushes. The dragon transformed back to Emily before I could make sense of what I was seeing. I slid down off her back as she swayed unsteadily. Then, from my sitting position, I could see the fountain.

Water no longer ran out of the mouth of the marble fish. In fact, the whole thing looked dried and cracked and overgrown with ivy, as though the place had been abandoned last summer. Someone had strung yellow police tape around the fountain, nailed boards across the bowl, and hung a sign around the fish. The sign said:

CLOSED FOR BUSINESS
NYAH-NYAH
(THAT MEANS YOU, EMILY AND GRACE PIZZELLI)

CHAPTER 16

Dear Someone . . .

I'M TOO TIRED to think," Emily said. "You tell me what to do."

I could see she wasn't exaggerating: She sank down to sitting, quickly, as though her legs had given out.

I didn't dare leave her for fear something in this world would get her, for fear she might weaken so much that if she fell asleep, I wouldn't be able to wake her up again. Not that I had any plan of action if I saw that start to happen.

"Rest a few minutes," I suggested. "Then we'll go in the house and get something to eat."

"Could you bring something for me?" she asked so plaintively I was tempted—except I didn't dare.

I grabbed her arm to keep her from lying down. "You'll be more comfortable indoors," I said, not wanting to share my fears—because I could only *hope* that strengthening her virtual self would give her real self more time. "Come on. Get up." I tugged at her. "Walking is easier than flying." I managed to haul her to her feet. "What's the route out of this maze?"

As though I needed evidence that she was muddled, Emily made several wrong turns.

"I can't think," she protested. "Just let me rest."

"No. Concentrate. The more you complain, the longer it will be till we get out of here."

Eventually, we made it—not only out of the maze, but across the lawn, up the porch stairs, and into the house. By then, Emily was leaning heavily on me, just as in one of those war paintings with titles like *Helping Her Wounded Comrade*.

I left Emily sitting in the library, for fear she'd fall right out of one of the kitchen chairs. "Stay awake," I told her, but I think she was asleep before I made it out of the room.

I was assuming I'd fetch the fastest-to-prepare meal I could find—maybe cereal, just to take the edge off our hunger before I took the time for something more substantial.

But when I opened one of the kitchen cupboards, it was filled with what appeared to be gift boxes, the kind with a bow on top for easy opening. It took a few moments for me to register that on their fronts were pictures of food. One shelf did indeed have boxes picturing cereal: Fruit Loops, Emily's favorite; but the boxes felt so light, I opened one up before even checking to see where the bowls were stored, just to make sure it wasn't empty. On the contrary, it held a bowl filled with Fruit Loops. There was even milk on the cereal already, and a spoon, as well as a linen nap-kin—the very picture that was on the front of the box. Talk about truth in advertising.

Still, *How long has this been sitting here?* I wondered. But when I took a spoonful, it was crunchy and fresh, as though the cold and frothy milk had been poured the moment I lifted the cover.

Interesting.

If that was the way things were . . .

I went to a different shelf and picked a box that had an image of a steaming slice of pepperoni pizza on it. And that—right down to the bubbling cheese—was what I found.

And the French toast box had thick slices of warm bat-tered bread with the flower-shaped pats of butter just be-ginning to melt and syrup that hadn't even thought of congealing yet. And the hot fudge sundae box had ice cream that was cold and firm, with the chocolate syrup warm and drippy, all looking as though it had been packed, like, one second before I opened the box. Each item came with its own appropriate dish and silverware, and a cloth napkin—in a variety of different colors and styles.

Okay, well, that was easier than hunting and gathering.

I loaded a bunch of boxes—including soda and hot cocoa with whipped cream—on a tray and brought it in to Emily.

She was asleep. I was grateful to hear her snoring, which

sounded like such an everyday normal thing. Surely the first step to fading isn't snoring.

But she did take some waking up. It was waving the pizza under her nose that finally got her to a sitting position.

She ate more than just a couple of mouthfuls, another reassurance.

I ate, too, a cheeseburger and fries. They were as yummy as could be, especially the fries, which were just the right balance of crunchy on the outside and squishy on the inside.

But now, all that done—Emily gotten back to the house, both of us fed a bit, rested a bit—now there was no putting off that it was time to come up with a plan.

And I didn't have one.

Why doesn't this stupid game come with a user's manual like the old-fashioned computer games? I thought. You know, the kind of thing to tell you: If the system crashes or freezes, press this button to turn the miserable piece-of-junk equipment off and reboot.

And that's when it suddenly hit me—Rasmussem games *do* come with a user's manual of sorts: the Finding Rasmussem Factor. Of course, with this game, which seemed designed mostly to encourage preteen girls to be shopaholic princesses, I didn't know if there even was the usual safety valve.

"Emily," I asked, "is there a Rasmussem to go to here?"

"What?" she asked groggily.

I shook her awake—or at least somewhat more awake—and repeated the question. I thought I was going to have to do it a third time, but apparently she'd been thinking.

"I don't know," she said. "That wasn't the area I was working on."

She seemed content to leave it at that, which I put down to her being one step removed from a stupor.

I asked, "How do I find the locals?"—which in this context meant a game character. There had, of course, been the gondolier, but even if he'd still been alive, any directions he might have rattled off would have been in Italian.

I fervently hoped sprites weren't the ones manning the help desk.

Emily said, "Write an invitation."

Was she getting delirious?

"What?" I asked.

"Go to the library . . ." Then she must have remembered we already were there. "Go to the roll-top desk," she amended. "Write a note inviting someone to come. Drop the envelope in the mail slot." She closed her eyes.

Invite someone. Never mind that I didn't know anyone's name. Let's see . . . there was hammock-swinging guy. Lute-playing guy. Throw-your-sister-out-of-your-party-then-toss-the-gondolier-to-his-death guy . . .

Except, of course, that Emily's guys were all foreign or mute.

Invite someone.

To something or other.

I went to the desk and found parchment and envelopes in the top drawer. There was one of those ostrich-feather pens and a bottle of ink, so I sat down and considered. I didn't want a whole mob of people, like there'd been at Emily's fancy ball. Nor did I want just one, in case that person turned out to be uncooperative. Once again the sprites came to mind, rising unwanted and unpleasant, like a burp after garlic mashed potatoes. The grandfather clock in the foyer obligingly chimed at that moment to remind me of its existence. From the doorway, I could see its face: three forty-five.

I picked up the plume, dipped it in the ink, and wrote:

To the first 5 young ladies of the land to receive this—
You are invited to Emily's house for English high tea
at 4 p.m. today.

This pen made my handwriting impeccable: both fancier and more legible than my usual, which my teachers certainly would have appreciated. My language could have been more formal, to go along with the graceful penmanship, so I made a little caret and added *cordially* to the *you are invited* line. The words shifted to make room.

To the first 5 young ladies of the land to receive this—
You are cordially invited to Emily's house
for English high tea at 4 p.m. today.

Please come.
Sincerely,
Grace Pizzelli

I folded the parchment in half, then stuck it in the envelope and looked around for the mail slot.

"Emily," I called. "Where does this go?"

But she was asleep.

I circled the room twice, and the grandfather clock was just going into its full on-the-hour routine before I noticed the cubbyhole in the desk itself that was labeled MAIL.

Somewhere between the music and the actual bonging of the hour, I flung the envelope into the cubbyhole. *Too late,* I thought. I'd cut the time too close. What I needed was to invite someone over for dinner at six—or even the next day. *If* that worked at all. Which it probably wouldn't.

But as soon as the clock finished its fourth bong, a doorbell rang.

A butler, complete with suit, white gloves, and a snooty expression, made it to the front door before me. Where'd he come from?

No matter; he opened the door and let in five young ladies, dressed as though they'd just stepped out of a Jane

Austen novel. It couldn't have been coincidence that they conveniently ranged from my age to Emily's.

"How kind of you to invite us," they said. And "My! What a charming house you and your sister have." And "That is such a beautiful dress you're wearing."

Well, all right, so they lost all credibility there, considering how dirty, sooty, and sweaty I was. I wondered how polite they'd be once they realized they had been invited under false pretenses, that there wasn't any tea prepared for them—high or otherwise.

They dropped their calling cards onto the little silver platter the butler presented for that purpose.

Was I supposed to read them, or were we pretending I actually knew who these girls were? Luckily, I didn't have to decide because a maid—a maid? Suddenly, we had servants coming out of the woodwork—held the library door open and curtsied and said, "This way, please, young misses."

In the fifteen or so seconds since I'd left the library, someone had brought in even more comfy chairs and arranged them—as well as the one in which Emily was still asleep—into a circle. And a coffee table had been set up— or rather, a tea table. There was a big silver pot, china cups and saucers, and trays that held small sandwiches, scones, and dessert-type goodies such as bite-sized fruit tarts, mini éclairs, cookies, and petits-fours. There were also more napkins, these monogrammed with a fancy *E*, since this was, after all, Emily's house.

"How lovely!" the girls cooed. And "Perfect!" and other such complimentary things.

"I'm glad you like everything," I said. "Please sit and enjoy. Meanwhile, I need to find out from you how to get to Rasmussem."

The girls, though still looking at me, though still— apparently—addressing me, somehow seemed to be ignoring me. They continued to stand, and they continued to murmur appreciatively about how fine everything looked.

Well, if we need Emily to ask before they'll answer, I thought, *we're out of luck.* I tried nudging my sister, but she just made grumpy sounds and shifted position. My visitors commented on how her dress suited her complexion.

The third time the maid cleared her throat, it finally occurred to me that maybe she didn't have a medical condition but was trying to tell me something. Once I glanced her way, I saw her shifting her eyes from me to one of the chairs. I *could* have assumed she had developed a twitch, but I'm a *bit* quicker than that. I sat, and that evidently was the girls' signal that they, too, could be seated.

"Will that be all, miss?" the maid asked me.

I don't know, I thought. *Is there anything else I need you to explain to me?* So I suggested, "Why don't you stay and join us."

The girls looked shocked, and the maid laughed as though I were the funniest person in the world. "Oh, Miss Grace. You are such a jokester."

Yeah, that's me.

But this explanation seemed to relieve my guests—that I simply had an odd sense of humor, which could be excused, rather than that I was scandalously common or insane. Invite a servant to sit with us! Evidently, that was Something That Is Not Done.

Okay. I nodded to the maid, and she curtsied and left.

"So," I tried with the girls again. "Rasmussem?"

But I guess I *did* still need the maid, for my guests didn't answer me, but instead declared how fine the weather was today, just as—it turned out—it had been fine yesterday, and—I learned—was due to be fine again tomorrow. Wow! Thrilling! Imagine that!

Nobody commented on Emily, still snoozing away.

And as yet nobody had touched the tea or goodies. I gathered that, just as good teatime manners must dictate that no one sit until the hostess does, perhaps they were waiting for me to get started. Maybe they would answer me once they were fed.

I seemed to be on the right track, because they all smiled and sat up a little straighter when I picked up the teapot. However, once I'd finished pouring a cup for myself and looked up, I could see little frowns on their faces, and the chatter about such scintillating subjects as how the blossoms on the trees seemed especially vibrant today—all that seemed to be faltering.

Okay, so I guess I'd once again failed in the manners

department. These overly sensitive girls wouldn't survive ten minutes in the Neil Armstrong High cafeteria.

What did I do wrong now?

This was so freaking crazy! All this time being frittered away, just to set up something I didn't even know for sure would work.

Calm, I told myself. Strangling one or more of my guests probably was *not* the key to getting them to cooperate.

Hmmm, clearly, *sit first* was correct, but not *serve myself first*.

I picked up my cup and saucer and passed them to the girl next to me, then held out my hand for the next, to show I'd pour for all. That must have been an adequate recovery, because they were willing to go with that, despite the sooty and blackberry-stained smudges my fingers left. I filled each of their cups, which they took while *still* looking right through me every time I asked, "Rasmussem?"— choosing, instead, to compliment me on the china and the tray linens. They kept using each other's names—"Aren't these chair pillows just divine, Chloe?" "Yes, Daphne, comfortable *and* beautifully embroidered"—which, I guess, was done for me to learn who was who.

Was this ever going to get me anywhere?

Enough already! I mentally screamed at them, though what I murmured was "Sugar?"

There was a brief silence.

"Helen?" I added, using one of the names I'd heard, though I wasn't sure who it went with.

"Oh, yes, please," said the girl next to me.

Then we did the whole one-lump-or-two routine and passed the cream, their spoons making that distinctive sound that comes when using good china rather than ordinary ceramic mugs. Seemingly, they were able to select their own sandwiches, which were all on mini buns or small croissants or slices of bread with the crusts removed. I took the one closest to me—which turned out to be cucumber and a really soft cheese. Nobody went for the desserts yet, although that would have been *my* inclination, which I guess just goes to show how naturally bad manners come to me.

Without even much hope at this point, I once again asked, "Rasmussem?"

"Yes, darling," said the girl the others called Beatrice. "What about it?"

It took a moment for me to realize she was responding to *me*, not to Chloe's statement that her smoked salmon sandwich was possibly the most delicious thing she'd ever tasted.

I jumped into the opportunity before it could close up and go away.

"Well," I said, "for starters, is Rasmussem a who, a what, or a where?"

"Yes," Zoe said with a giggle. Zoe and Chloe were twins.

Chloe was the slightly fussy one; Zoe said *everything* with a giggle.

Chloe expanded on her sister's answer. "Rasmussem is the name of the amusement arcade run by the gypsies. It's also the name of the gypsy king who owns and operates the fair."

"Where is it?" I asked, and, before we even moved on to the scones, my guests—now that I'd been the proper hostess—explained to me exactly how to get there.

CHAPTER 17

Finding Rasmussem

Excuse me," I said to the Jane Austen fan club, setting my teacup down. I stood and moved over to where Emily slouched napping in her chair. "Emily."

She looked alert a lot more quickly than she had any other time that day, so maybe the food and the rest had done her good. She gave a little wave to the girls, as though not at all confused or surprised to see we had guests. For their part, the girls watched us with quizzical, suspicious expressions that I was sure covered the thought: *What's this socially inept person going to do now?*

"Emily," I said, "we've got a plan."

"Okay," she answered. "Do you need me?"

No way was I leaving her behind. "Yes," I said.

She even got up by herself. Sure, she needed a little bit of steadying—but I no longer felt like I was trying to prod a bag of kitty litter into moving.

"Enjoy the rest of the tea," I told the Austenites. "Ring for the maid if you need anything else."

They didn't say a word. They were too polite, and they didn't have to. Their appalled faces said it all: never had they witnessed anything so unspeakably atrocious as a hostess abandoning her own tea party.

I was ready to run, but Emily was moving at more of a moseying pace. Then, when we got to the foyer, she made to go up the stairs.

"What are you doing?"

"I'm all grimy and nasty," she said. "It'll only take a few minutes to shower and change."

"No," I said. "That's just . . . frivolous."

Frivolous? When had I become the kind of person who would say something that sounded so . . . so like our mother? Even if I *was* right.

We compromised by washing our hands and faces, taking off the top layer of dirt. I have to admit my spirits felt inordinately lifted for it, and I realized I probably should have taken the time to rinse off my hands in the kitchen before eating. Besides the boost to my morale, my food might not have been so gritty. I looked down at my wrinkled, sweaty, sooty, blackberry-stained dress. I knew it would feel a lot better to get out of those clothes, but it would feel better yet to get out of this treacherous game altogether, so I settled for exchanging my remaining, almost-worn-through silver ballet flat for a pair of sparkly flip-flops from Emily's closet, the only footwear she had that more or less fit my smaller foot.

Once we were ready, Emily asked, "Where are we going?"

"Into the forest," I told her. "From what the girls said, I'm gathering Rasmussem is somewhere beyond where the unicorn was." Then, because I wasn't sure how many unicorns there were, I added, "You know, the clearing where that guy was playing the lute for you."

Emily considered. "So, near the arcade?"

I sighed in exasperation.

"What?" she asked.

"It didn't occur to you, when I said we needed to find Rasmussem, that we might try the Rasmussem Arcade?"

Emily shrugged. "I didn't know the place had a name. Should I turn into a dragon to take us there?"

It would save time, but transformations seemed to wipe Emily out. I could *hope*, but I couldn't *count on* her newfound strength lasting. "We'll walk," I told her.

"Walking seems like a lot of effort," Emily said, following me to the front door. "Is there some special reason we shouldn't take the horses?"

I stopped so quickly, she bumped into me.

Naturally, there were horses. Don't little girls love horses?

We went outside, and Emily whistled. Two times. After a moment, I heard a whinny. Then the clomping of hooves. Two horses—one black, the other gray—came around the corner of the house. Conveniently, they were bridled and saddled.

The only problem was that the last time I'd ridden had been at the Monroe County Fair so long ago that Emily and I had been together on the same horse. And actually, it had been a pony. For a dollar, the 4-H club girls had lifted us onto its back and led us around a ring.

These horses were big. Big feet. Big legs. Big chests. Big teeth.

"Yikes," I said. I mean, I'm guessing they were normal size as horses go, but you get used to them looking a lot smaller when the only time you see them is in far-off fields rather than right next to you, stomping their feet restively.

"They act very spirited, but they won't bite, buck, kick, or try to knock you off with a low branch," Emily reassured me, patting the head and neck of the black horse as if they were old friends.

"Oh, good," I said. "Those were things I didn't even know to worry about."

Both horses got down on the ground for easy mounting—a nice change from dragon riding. Clearly, the game's developers realized that a lot more little girls *love* horses than really have ever had any dealings with them. Once we were ready, our mounts eased back up to standing a lot more smoothly than I believe is actually physically possible.

If horses even can lower themselves like that. Which they probably can't.

Anyway, Emily took the lead, and my horse followed hers, both moving at a trot. I think. I'm not a horsey person, so I'm not sure. Any little girl would have sat there happy and confident, never imagining that she might fall off. The trouble is: I have a much better imagination than your average little girl.

I was holding on so tightly, I didn't even reach out for the butterflies that fluttered around us as we rode through the forest, offering themselves up for ready cash, though Emily did.

Making much better time than we would have walking, we reached the clearing with lute-guy in about ten minutes. Even though Emily hadn't been there in at least twenty-four hours, he was still strumming away, singing a song in Latin. Nothing beats those popular tunes from around the time of the fall of Rome. He didn't acknowledge us passing through, except to gaze at Emily adoringly.

I was stiff because my anxiety had made me tighten up, but I think it was really only about another ten minutes until I could once again hear music. For about half a second I worried that we'd gone around in a circle and come back to lute-guy. But this melody was much more energetic. And a totally different sound. Another half second and I realized that we were hearing a calliope, one of those old-fashioned organ-and-drum contraptions that are part of vintage merry-go-rounds, the ones from the late eighteen hundreds. It was playing "Stars and Stripes Forever."

We had found the arcade.

Less than a minute later, we came to it.

And, excuse me, Emily, but there was a big banner to mark the entry that said:

RASMUSSEM ARCADE WELCOME!

First impression, while we were still approaching on our horses: it looked like a cross between a Renaissance Faire and a Victorian amusement park.

The carousel was front and center. It wasn't huge, but it had an assortment of brightly painted animals, including a zebra, a cheetah, a lion, an ostrich. Lots of detail. Embellishments. Gemstones. Manes and tails and feathers that fluttered in the wind as the animals went around and around and up and down.

Meandering paths of sparkly crushed pastel stones wound among the trees and led to more rides, and to wooden booths protected from the sun by colorful awnings.

Emily may have wobbled a bit dismounting, or that might have been my imagination, or it might have been that *I* wobbled a bit getting down.

We left the horses without tethering them; Emily assured me they would wait for us however long we took.

My hope, naturally, was that we wouldn't need them, that we would find a ready way to shut the game down in the next couple minutes. But just in case, it was good to know the horses wouldn't wander away.

There were park benches and Adirondack rockers placed all around in case anyone grew weary from all the fun, and I wished we could have spared the time for a good long rest for Emily. But the fact that she already looked like she could use one proved that there *was* no time.

Once we walked past the merry-go-round, I saw that the booths held an assortment of games of chance or stuff for sale: wind chimes, hammocks, Ren-Faire clothing, jewelry, stuffed animals that were as big as toddlers, decorative mirrors, food.

Food. The air was thick with the smell of cotton candy, popcorn, and those greasy but fabulous fried dough things sold at amusement parks.

The people who were enjoying the rides and the games were mostly dressed like they were from the eighteen hundreds: parasol-carrying women in white lawn dresses, men in elegant light-colored suits and top hats—which was what gave the place the Victorian amusement park feel. On the other hand, the people running the rides or manning the booths were the very stereotype of gypsies: the women in many-hued flounced skirts, hoop earrings, and bangles; the men with small, brightly colored scarves tied at their necks. It was these workers who gave the arcade its Ren-Faire atmosphere. Since I actually enjoy that sort of thing, this setting wasn't as in-your-face annoying as other places I'd been in this game. Which didn't make our situation any less desperate.

As was typical in this world, the women were laughing and talking; the guys were there mostly to add visual interest. Except, on closer observation, the gypsy men were able to speak—just not English: I heard snatches of what might well have been German and Hawaiian, and that funny clicking, whistling language of the African bushmen.

"If the gypsy king isn't female," I said to Emily, "this conversation is going to be difficult."

"Oops," Emily said.

A fat lot of help *oops* was. I could only guess Emily's fatigue had made her punchy.

We passed a fire eater (no wonder *he* wasn't talking, what with the scorched larynx and all) and a juggler, then we came to a woman doing acrobatics from these huge silk scarves that hung from a massive oak tree—very Cirque de Soleil.

"Excuse me," I called out to her. "We're looking for . . . um . . ." What *was* the proper title for gypsy royalty? ". . . King Rasmussem?"

At that point, the acrobat was hanging upside down, supported only by a twist of fabric around her ankle as she spun in spirals. "Beyond the Theatre in the Grove," she told us, "turn at the llamas, go on to the Big Wheel."

Llamas?

I was about to ask her if the Big Wheel was a ride or a game when something dropped down directly in front of us. For a second, I thought the acrobat had fallen. But it was a man dressed as a jester who had jumped from another branch in the same tree. He landed on both feet, then stood there with his arms wide as though expecting applause. Even though he didn't get any, he made elaborate gestures, like, *No, no, please, I'm too modest to accept such acclaim.*

Emily and I would have gone around him, but he walked backwards, remaining in our way, pretending that he was using a broom to sweep our path clear, then pretending that he was scattering flower petals before us.

Great. A mime. Talk about the worst of silent men.

I tried to maneuver us around him, but he zigzagged exasperatingly to keep blocking us, now pretending to pull coins from our ears.

"We're in a rush," I told the guy. "We don't have time for this foolishness."

He put his hand to his ear, as though he were hard of hearing as well as mute.

"Please move out of our way," I said, speaking more loudly.

Again with the ear gesture.

"This is important!" I practically screamed at him. "Your delays are life threatening!" They were. I thought I was very diplomatic because I refrained from adding "as well as being infuriating, pointless, and just generally stupid."

The mime pulled off his ear—well, *an* ear; it was rubber—and he looked at it as though trying to figure out why it didn't work. He tapped it. Shook it. Then tossed it over his shoulder with a shrug and a smile.

Emily laughed, proof that she was getting too tired to think straight.

Okay, maybe the mime was related to the sprites. I handed him a gold coin.

He made it disappear into his own ear, then held his hand out for another.

Greedy thing. I handed him a second coin, which he made disappear into his other ear. And now he held out his first hand again.

I gave him two coins, which he made disappear up his nose, and that's just downright nasty. Plus, now he held out both hands.

I was ready to scream at the endless delaying, but knew that wasn't going to help.

Instead, I put my hand on Emily's arm and held up my index finger to the mime, signaling them both to wait a moment. I went through my own pantomime, as though I'd found something on the ground. I bent to pick it up. By holding my hands together, then spreading them out, I showed that what I was holding was long, long, long, and thin: a rope. I handed one end of this rope to the mime; then I quickly walked around and around him at least a dozen times, going from his shoulders down to his ankles, where I showed that I was firmly tucking the other end of the rope in. Lastly, I dusted off my hands and nodded firmly.

True to the mime code of conduct, the guy stood there writhing as though in a cocoon of rope, and Emily and I were able to step around him.

"You're just a little bit weird, Grace," Emily said.

I gave an exaggerated, mimelike shrug. It was that, or kick her for not taking this seriously enough.

We came to a bunch of enormous, big-enough-to-sit-on toadstools, arranged in rows in front of a raised platform that was obviously a stage. A sign by the path announced:

Theatre in the Grove
Madrigal Singers
appearing in:
1 minute, 47 seconds

As we approached, the 47 changed to 46, then 45, the sign functioning as if it had a digital readout even though it looked like old-fashioned painted wood.

"Oooo," Emily said, "I love madrigal music."

Not good, I thought. *Not good, not good.* Emily knew the danger. Her lack of focus frightened me.

I held tight to her arm lest she veer off.

Emily pouted but didn't complain.

We passed some more booths that housed arcade-style games, some older (throw the hatchet at the bull's-eye target), some newer (video tic-tac-toe). Most seemed to offer winners a choice, either gold coins or an actual prize. And the prizes weren't like the stuff you usually see at carnivals: Mardi Gras beads or plastic airplanes or goldfish in a bowl. These guys were offering things like silver-and-crystal tiaras, and bicycles, and puppies.

"Very generous arcade," I commented.

"Yeah, well," Emily said, "I don't like to wait."

"You don't like to wait?" I repeated, not clear about what she meant.

"The way games start slow, and you've got to build up experience points before you can do anything worthwhile. Or like at a carnival, where you win crappy little things, and you have to trade up to the good stuff."

That's what happens, I thought, *to someone who's always gotten everything effortlessly.*

And I remembered the sprites being mad about how she'd changed things to make the game easier.

"Nice," I said, but I was thinking: *Sure, winning is more fun than losing, but what's the point if you KNOW you're going to win?*

As we came to a petting zoo enclosure, Emily told me, "You *have* to hold the chinchilla. You won't believe how soft it is."

"Maybe next time," I said, feeling I'd completed the transformation into our mother.

The path divided, and we turned after the last enclosure, the one with the baby llamas standing by the fence as though just waiting for us to pet them.

Emily's steps were beginning to falter, whether from fatigue or from forgetting what we were supposed to be doing and being tempted to cuddle the animals. Not a good sign in either case.

"King Rasmussem?" I asked the gypsy worker who was handing out large rubber rings for people to toss over small bowling pins set conveniently close to the counter.

With a nod of his head, he indicated farther down the row.

And there we were. At the Big Wheel. It was one of those wooden contraptions divided into skinny pie pieces, each with a number. The operator was a guy, which meant communication could be a problem, given my lack of knowledge of foreign languages. He didn't look royal. But on the other hand, he also didn't look like the other people I'd seen in this game, most of whom leaned toward young and attractive. He was about our dad's age, a bit short, a bit gray, and carrying a bit too much weight. He had a black mustache and was wearing a T-shirt that said: *The voices in my head are generally friendly.*

Which was somewhat reassuring. And somewhat not.

"Hello," I said.

"Bonjour," he answered.

Drat.

Hopefully, I continued, "We're looking for King Rasmussem."

"Le roi, c'est moi."

He was speaking what sounded like French (I mean, even little kids know *bonjour*), but because his shirt was in English, I hoped maybe he could understand me better than I was understanding him.

"Do you speak English?" I asked.

Instead of answering, he spun the wheel.

Round and round it went, clicking first quickly, then slowly, until it finally stopped at 100, the largest number.

If that was supposed to be an answer, I didn't get it.

I saw that the next booth over was one of those rides for really little kids, with a bunch of boats that go around in a large tub of water that is always green and somewhat funky. When I'd been the right age for that ride, I'd been convinced the water was actual seawater.

The ride operator was a gypsy girl not much older than me, looking bored because the boats were currently empty. I ran up to her and asked with a tilt of my head, "Is that the king of the gypsies at the Big Wheel?"

"Yes," she said.

"Do you speak whatever language he's speaking?"

"It's French," she told me.

"Right. Do you speak French?"

"Mais oui," she said.

I wanted to say, "Come on, come on—can't you talk any faster?" Instead, I asked, "Can you translate for me?"

She held her hand out, and—after ten or twenty seconds—I caught on and gave her my next-to-last butterfly coin. She came back with me to good King Big Wheel.

Emily was sitting on the ground, leaning her back against the booth.

"You okay?" I asked.

"Never better," she answered, but I didn't believe her for a second.

"Bonjour," the gypsy girl said to the king.

He smiled and nodded and said something like, "Ahnyahng hah say-o." Which sure didn't sound French to me.

"Oh, dear," gypsy girl said. "Now he's speaking Korean. I don't speak Korean." She obviously wasn't devastated by this development. She put the coin I'd given her on the counter. But before I could marvel at the thought that she was actually refunding my money since she was unable to translate, Gypsy King Rasmussem took the coin and gave the wheel a spin. It landed on the 100 again. The girl gave him a thumbs-up, a *good job* gesture, which he returned.

"I hate to interrupt all these festivities, but is there anyone here, besides the king, who speaks Korean?" I asked her. "We *need* to talk to him."

She looked around, then pointed at a man who was giving little kids rides on a huge, saddled pig.

"Okay," I said, but I'd been in this game long enough to ask, "But does he speak English?"

"No." Gypsy girl grinned and added, "But he does speak French."

"This is ridiculous," I complained. "You mean I have to ask my questions in English, you'll repeat them in French, that man there will ask King Rasmussem in Korean, and then we'll have to do the same thing in reverse for the king's answer?"

"Shouting at me isn't going to make this take any less time."

I sighed. I looked at Emily, who shrugged. I looked at King Rasmussem of the Odd T-Shirt, who smiled. I looked at the pig man, who was just helping the last of a group of children to dismount from the pig.

"All right," I told her.

"And of course," Gypsy girl said, "you'll need to pay both of us."

"I already paid you!"

Patiently, she explained, "You paid me to translate back and forth between you and the king. Now you need to pay me to translate back and forth with the pig man."

"Emily," I said, "I need coins."

She dug into her pocket and gave me a small handful.

Gypsy girl waved pig man over.

I gave him one of the coins, and he plunked it down in front of King Rasmussem, who spun the wheel. It stopped, rather predictably by now, on 100.

Pig man and King Rasmussem bumped fists in congratulations.

"Ask," I said to the girl, "if he can help us get out of the game."

Gypsy girl said something to pig man; pig man said something to King Rasmussem; King Rasmussem said something to pig man; pig man said something to gypsy girl; gypsy girl turned to me and said, "You took too long and missed his Korean phase. He's into Polish now."

I slammed my hand down hard on the counter of the booth. "No! That's not fair!"

King Rasmussem folded his arms across his chest and said, "Well, it's your own damn fault. You and that cheater sister of yours."

CHAPTER 18

The Big Wheel

H EY!" I cried in a combination of relief and exasperation. "You speak English!"

King Rasmussem bared his teeth at me, an expression I didn't for a second confuse with a smile or friendliness.

"But Emily made it so the guys here . . ." I hesitated. Did the game characters *know* they were game characters? I looked to my sister for advice, but she was still sitting, leaning against the booth, yawning so big it looked like she was trying to swallow her hand. I worked on amending my thought midsentence, and in the meantime King Rasmussem finished it for me.

"She made it so that the guys in the Land of the Golden Butterflies can't speak English. But how helpful would a Rasmussem Help function be if it was in a different language from the one used by the consumer?" He said something in some language I hadn't heard yet—Romany, maybe?—to the French gypsy and the Korean gypsy, and they both laughed.

At me, I was sure.

"So what was all that about?" I demanded. "With the different languages?" Even to myself, I sounded like a sulky whiner. And in the end: so what? That wasn't important. Getting out of here—*that* was important.

"Just having fun," King Rasmussem said. "Isn't an arcade supposed to be fun?"

"That was not fun," I corrected him. "That was annoying—that was like annoying to the tenth power—and it was time-consuming, and frustrating. And dangerous, given how vital it is that we talk to you."

"My mistake," King Rasmussem said. "That's what happens with artificial intelligence sometimes—there are misunderstandings."

So he did know he was a game character. Sort of.

"Okay," I said, not believing that *misunderstanding* began to cover what we'd just been through, but—again—so what? "Well, what we came here for was to find out why the End Game/Return to Rasmussem function doesn't work."

"Ah!" His tone indicated pleased surprise—like a teacher's, when you ask the question he wants you to ask. "Well . . ." The gypsy king launched into an explanation. I guess. It took like about ten whole seconds before I realized he was speaking technobabble and not yet another language.

"Stop, stop, stop!" I interrupted. "I don't understand a word you're saying."

"Oh," he told me, "that's not true. Tangent. Greater than. Underscore. Backslash—"

"All right, all right," I interrupted again. "The individual words I get, but what—"

It was his turn to interrupt. "Code," he explained. "You told me you wanted to find out why the game isn't working the way you think it should, and I'm telling you the code responsible for that malfunction."

I leaned against the counter to move in closer to him. "I'm not interested in the code."

He leaned in, too, so that we were practically nose to nose. "You said you were."

This could be enough to turn me off games forever. "I *meant*," I said, fighting through the urge to shake him, "we want to go home *now*."

"But that's not what you said."

"That's what I'm saying at this moment."

"Too late." Once again he bared his teeth, and this was much more a smile than before. Not that it was friendly. He was inordinately pleased with himself, and I suspected that was not a good sign.

"By *too late*," I asked, "do you mean you're committed to reciting the entire computer code to me?"

"Nooo." He was having too good a time with this, obviously filled with glee at how the conversation was going. Well, at least one of us was entertained. "By *too late*, I mean your sister has meddled too much."

Emily roused herself enough to protest, "Hey." But not with much enthusiasm. She looked barely able to keep her eyes open, and she didn't even try to stand.

On the other hand, I found King Rasmussem's words chilling. "Who says?" I asked, trying to make my voice self-assured and forceful, rather than scared. "So what?"

"As artificial constructs," King Rasmussem said, "we are given enough intelligence to fill in the gaps."

"Huh?" I said.

"With early versions of computer games, the player had to use the exact wording the designers had anticipated or the program was unable to respond. A programmer would have to try to cover a variety of ways a player might phrase a request; for example, 'Pick up the sword,' or 'Get the sword,' or 'Lift the sword.' If a player happened to choose a phrase the programmer hadn't thought of . . . say, 'Take hold of the sword,' the game would freeze. Unsatisfying for everyone. For a smooth user-machine interface, the machine needs to make leaps of logic—the way people do."

"Yeah," I said, "but—"

The king kept on talking. "Think of how getting one character wrong in an e-mail address means that your gazillion-gigabyte computer has no idea where to send your letter. But your average-intelligence, just-three-more-years-till-retirement postal carrier can figure out that '317 Main' means '317 Main Street,' and that 'Roch., NY' means 'Rochester, New York.' And if the zip code is written '19611' instead of '14611,' which is Reading, Pennsylvania—and not Rochester, New York, at all—a human being, or artificial intelligence, can surmise what was probably meant."

"Okay," I said. "But I can't surmise what you mean." It was too good a line to pass up—*and* it was true.

King Rasmussem crinkled his face in a semblance of good humor. "I *mean* we're ticked off at the way your sister has been cheating like crazy, so we're not going to let you out of the game until the two of you can finish a task without cheating."

He was a game character. Could he do that?

Well, duh, he already had or we'd be home by now.

Artificial intelligence was still intelligence, so I appealed to reason. "But Emily has been in the game too long already. She *needs* to get out."

Once again the king leaned forward till we were nose to nose. "And I *need* her to do so without cheating. I'm stripping her of her magic, her ill-gotten possessions, her servants. I'm setting the number of butterflies back to a level that does *not* indicate an infestation. I'm making the games of chance once more involve . . ." He paused for dramatic effect. "Chance."

Emily was rummaging through her pockets. "Hey," she said again, this time with an edge of annoyance.

I felt my pocket for the small stash she had given me. Gone. The gold coins had changed into wooden nickels. Every bit as eloquent as my sister, I, too, said, "Hey!" Then I protested, "I haven't cheated."

The king snorted. "As good as: you accepted help from a cheater."

Now *I* was ticked. "Yeah?" I said to the king. "Like this wheel of yours that always comes up a hundred isn't cheating?"

"My wheel," King Rasmussem said, "is now and always has been working exactly as it's meant to." He reached into the pouch where he kept his coins and plunked two down on the counter that separated us. "Gifts," he said. "One for Miss Grace. One for Miss Emily. Go ahead. Try the wheel."

I was tempted to just take my coin and leave. But what good was one gold coin? And where could we go? Finding Rasmussem had been a last resort. Emily was failing, and if we didn't play along with the king, did we even have another option?

With no idea what the king's point was, I touched one of the coins to acknowledge possession of it. "Sure. Why not?" I slid the coin toward him.

He took the coin and spun the wheel.

click click click click click

Then slower.

click   click   click

Then slower.

click   click

Then one final *click*.

The wheel had stopped at 87.

Well, at least that was different.

I had no idea what it meant, but it was different.

"Not a bad score," King Rasmussem said. "Not as high as us make-believe people. But not bad."

"So . . . ?" I asked. His booth consisted of the wheel and the counter to separate us from the wheel. There were no numbers on the counter, so we weren't betting on what would come up, and there were no shelves with prizes—neither exorbitant nor conventional. Had I just won eighty-seven pieces of our gold back? But he hadn't given any coins to the gypsy girl or the pig man when he'd spun for them. "What do I win?"

The king and the gypsies exchanged a bemused look over that. "You won an eighty-seven," the king said.

Before I could say, "Wow! That *IS* exciting!" I became aware that Emily was standing directly behind me. She had pulled herself up to see what was going on as the wheel spun.

Now she put her hand over the remaining coin. "Since you took all of mine, I should keep this," she said. "Spend it on something useful." Same thought I had had. Which maybe showed that we were more alike than I thought. Or maybe it just showed that this interminable game had made us both cranky.

In any case, King Rasmussem shrugged.

Emily lifted her hand off the coin, hesitated a second,

then pushed it forward with the heel of her palm. She kept both her hands on the counter—I suspected that was to keep herself steady.

Once more the king spun the wheel.

It landed at 22.

Suddenly, without any idea what was going on, I had a very bad feeling about this.

"Oooo," the king said, sounding impressed, but certainly not in a good way. Sounding like when someone says "Oooo, so how long did your parents ground you for?" or "Oooo, that burn looks as though it hurts," or "Oooo, that girl in the movie should definitely *not* go to investigate the noise in the basement."

"Oooo," the other two gypsies echoed.

"That *is* low," the king told us. His voice gave away that he was tickled to be the bearer of unfortunate news.

"Twenty-two *what*?" I demanded.

"Twenty-two on the life scale," King Rasmussem said. He leaned forward and spoke to Emily in a loud whisper. "Better put your life in order, Emily Pizzelli. There isn't time for much else."

CHAPTER 19

By Royal Decree

I PURPOSELY AVOIDED looking at Emily's face.

"*See?*" I said to King Rasmussem, still expecting—I have no idea why—to find sense in this game. "We need to get out of here. We don't have time to play anymore. Emily is sorry she cheated—tell him you're sorry, Emily."

I finally did steal a glance at her, and saw that her face was gray, and she was shaking. I'm guessing the same was probably true for me. She'd spun 22 out of 100. How much time did that translate to?

Barely above a whisper, Emily agreed, "I *am* sorry," as I continued, "We're both sorry. And if you want, we can come back later, or we can promise never to come back—whichever you prefer. Because, really, you have been wronged here, there's no denying that. It's just that now is not a good time. Which your wheel has just verified." My babbling, and I admit I was babbling, petered out. It wasn't that the king wasn't reacting—he was reacting with boredom.

Flatly, he said, "Huzzah," which is Ren-Faire-speak for "Hurray." As with *hurray*, how you say it can be a good indication of your sincerity level. I'd guess the king's sincerity hovered somewhere around . . . NOT.

He said, "So you admit your guilt?"

"Yes," Emily whispered.

"Yes," I said.

The king gave me a long, level look. "You just denied being a cheater not two minutes ago."

"But you explained it to me," I said, eager to be forgiven. "Now I see that I *am* guilty. Because I knew she had modified the code so she could have more money and wishes, and yet I accepted money from her. I'm an accomplice after the fact. A guilty cheater accomplice, that's me."

The king turned back to Emily. "And you're remorseful over this cheating?"

"Yes," Emily said.

"Definitely remorseful," I agreed.

"And you're willing to prove this?"

Emily and I exchanged a worried look.

"Prove?" Emily repeated.

"What do you mean, *prove*?" I asked. I glanced at gypsy girl and pig man and didn't see anything reassuring in their faces.

"You will work to accomplish the task I give you, even though I have removed the code you wrote, the code that made things easier?"

"Excuse me," I said. "Isn't that what you said before?"

"Yes."

"Then what have you changed now that Emily and I have confessed and apologized?"

"Nothing."

Some negotiation. "So what," I asked, trying not to let my anger show, "did apologizing accomplish?"

King Rasmussem considered. "Did it make you feel better?" he suggested.

I was tempted to say *no*, but figured that couldn't improve the situation and might conceivably make things worse, because then the king would accuse me of being a guilty cheater *liar.* Grudgingly, I admitted, "Yes," and dug my elbow into Emily's side.

"Yes," she echoed, playing along.

"Huzzah," the king said—also playing along, because we all knew, he didn't believe us for a second.

Her voice raspy, Emily asked, "What, exactly, is the task you're setting for us?"

"Return your ill-gotten gains to the sprites."

"What do you mean?" I asked.

"Miss Emily set the golden butterflies to come every five minutes rather than once an hour. She set the flowers in the flower-match garden game to grow back as soon as they were cut off rather than the next day. She set the prices of the articles she wanted to buy from the sprites too low, and made the market dwarves accept the ridiculously high prices of the articles she wanted to sell. She set the arcade games to be won too easily, and the prizes to be too grand. She—"

"Yes, yes," Emily said. Despite her general fogginess, despite her obvious fear, more than anything she sounded out of patience. "I cheated. I admitted that."

"By my calculation, you have accrued 87,853 more gold coins than even the most diligent and attentive player *could* have. And you"—he turned to me—"owe the sprites 7 coins."

Had I missed something?

"Excuse me?"

"Seven." The king spun the wheel and it landed on 7.

"Huzzah," the gypsy girl and the pig man said.

"Yeah, but . . ." Well, I certainly shouldn't be putting ideas in anybody's head—but how had he calculated seven when I'd taken that chest of jewelry and gems from Emily's pavilion and used that to bargain with the sprites?

The king gave his zero-degree-Fahrenheit smile. "You're thinking about that money you stole from your sister."

Now Emily was looking at me, too. "You did what?"

"Well . . ." I said.

"That wasn't cheating," the king said. "That was gamesmanship. And the trades you made with the sprites—you were working with the game as your sister had changed it."

Well, as long as he was cutting me so much slack . . . I asked, "So which seven coins are you counting against me?"

"The seven you asked for and received right here in front of me. That was knowing receipt of stolen goods."

"Okay," I said. Not that it made any difference. Getting seven coins was accomplishable; eighty-seven-thousand-whatever was not. But it wasn't like I was going to abandon Emily.

Emily asked, "Where are we going to get eighty-eight thousand coins?"

"Don't exaggerate," the king said. "It's 87,853."

"Whatever."

"Well, let's see. There's always a golden butterfly when you first arrive, and since I just reset the game for the two of you . . ."

I snatched at the glittery little thing that I suddenly realized was hovering around my shoulder. Emily, with sluggish reactions, missed the one that alighted on the counter. It rose back up into the air—and the gypsy girl caught it.

"Hey!" Emily protested.

"You should have been quicker," the girl told her.

"Don't worry," the king said. "Another pair will come by in fifty-nine and a half minutes."

"It'll take *years* to earn enough money two butterflies at a time," I said.

King Rasmussem looked at me as though I had spaghetti coming out my nose. "What are you thinking?" he asked, as though I'd said I *wanted* to play for years. "Your sister doesn't *have* years."

What I was thinking involved my hands, his throat, and squeezing, but I didn't think this was a good thought to share.

"Do you have any suggestions?" I asked as pleasantly as I could.

As though it were a big revelation, he recommended, "Get more coins faster."

The pleasantness got even more strained as my favorite mental image grew more vivid. I repeated, "Do you have any suggestions?"

"Well, let's see . . ." The king paused as though considering. "Who has a lot of gold coins?"

I assumed it was a rhetorical question, but the gypsy girl said, "The sprites."

Pig man, with his newfound ability to speak English, added, "Except they've run out because of"—he nodded toward Emily, as though she and I weren't standing right there watching and listening—"you-know-who."

"Hmmm," the king said, still playing at being the thoughtful helper.

"Dragons," Emily blurted out, surprising me because I'd written her off as being no help at all. "Dragons always have gold."

"Huzzah," the gypsies cheered.

CHAPTER 20

Go Back to "Go"

Dragons?" I repeated. "Where are there dragons? Present company excepted, of course, seeing as we've both lost our magical ability . . ." Using the word *lost* was a politeness on my part, since I felt *stolen away* was more strictly accurate.

The king shrugged expansively.

"Mountains," Emily said. She sighed. "Back where we came from. I've seen them swooping over the mountain peaks."

"Wonderful," I muttered. It wasn't that our trip away from the mountains had been useless, since we hadn't had all the information we needed when we'd been back there. But it had taken us all day to get this far—and that had been flying. "Any advice on how to get there?" I asked.

Again the king shrugged, with a helpless smile. It was as though the English language had suddenly dribbled out of his brain—either that or his IQ had dropped forty points.

"Anyone?"

Gypsy girl and pig man followed the king's lead and gave their own shrugs.

"There's no way," Emily told me. "It can't be done. I'll help you gather those seven coins you need, and then *you* can go home."

"Not without you," I told her. I was remembering when I'd been seven years old and I was afraid of some of the older kids at the school bus stop. Dad tried to convince me I could ignore them, and Mom offered to talk to their mothers. Emily had made a game of it. We were superheroes, with powers that changed at our whim. We needed to maintain our secret identities, which those middle schoolers were too dumb to see through. But if we needed to, we could always use our superpowers. Once I was no longer afraid, the middle schoolers lost interest.

Fortified by this memory, I repeated more forcefully, "I'm not leaving without you."

"We'll see," Emily said.

She'd given up.

That *We'll see* was a delaying trick our mother sometimes used, and that thought brought Mom to mind—Mom waiting at Rasmussem, watching those readouts, growing more anxious by the moment. She'd been like two and a half seconds from a meltdown when we'd been assuring her that both Emily and I could get out of the game any time we wanted to.

"I have a plan," I told Emily.

She didn't look hopeful. She didn't even look particularly interested. But she asked, "What?"

"I'll tell you as we walk back to your place," I said, unwilling to talk in front of King Rasmussem.

Which made little if any sense, considering that the entire game was going on in my head, and he was in there, too.

But I didn't want to look at his smug face anymore.

"Come on." I pulled on Emily's arm, and she shuffled along beside me. Past the boat ride, past the petting zoo, past the spot where I'd tied up the mime. (Either he'd been reset, too, when the king reinstated the original code, or someone had rescued him, because he was gone.) Cirque du Soleil lady was still doing her thing with the scarves. The merry-go-round was playing a jaunty carnival tune and had turned its lights on, because the sun was only a handspan or two above the horizon. At this point, I felt the lights gave the arcade a look that wasn't so much festive as sinister.

Of course Emily's horses had disappeared just as surely as her gold and her magic had. So that's how we came to be walking through the forest, heading toward her house. Along the way we each captured two more butterflies, which was one of those good news/bad news things: good, because we could use all the gold coins we could get; bad, because that goes to show what incredibly slow progress we were making, with Emily needing to sit down frequently. The sky still had a bit of pink when we got to the first clearing, which was *just* a clearing: no sign of lute-guy, since he had been conjured up by Emily. By the time we got to the second clearing, night had fallen.

There was a full moon—according to Emily, there was a full moon every night—and that gave enough light to show that the forest ended at an expanse of lawn. Only a few wildflowers dotted the grass—no garden in this new scaled-down version of the game, so no flower-matching game. No gazebo. The topiary maze was still there, since that's where the sprites' fountain was, but the king had warned us that the sprites wouldn't come back till we went to their homeland with the gold we owed them. Probably all for the best. I don't think I was mentally up to the challenge of dealing with them. And Emily's house? Her fine Victorian mansion had returned to its default setting, no upgrades, just a plain little cobblestone cottage with a thatched roof. We had gone back to basics. It had one door, one window. The flower box beneath the window was empty.

Inside the cottage, the floor was concrete, like a garage. One big room. The stones the place was constructed with made bare walls, the same inside as out. A toilet and sink were set off in the corner behind a wooden partition. There were two sleeping bags on the floor, one for each of us. To add insult to injury, they were that ugly green of surplus army equipment.

"See?" Emily said. "I hate entry-level games."

Certainly not rich accommodations, but we weren't planning on spending much time here. As I had explained to Emily while we walked, we had to get a dragon to come to us, since there was no way we could reach the mountains where they made their dens, not without magic, not in the time Emily had left.

"It's not going to work," Emily had said.

I had gone to that old family fallback position of "We'll see," because I didn't want to argue with her. I was getting tired of her being tired, and of me having to be the responsible one. When was it going to be *my* turn to get to be tired? A cranky little part of my brain kept repeating that we were in this bad situation because of Emily, and it was hard not to let my irritation spill over.

The last thing I needed was Emily feeling sorry for herself. It infringed on *my* feeling sorry for *myself*.

I opened the food cupboard and saw that the entire stock of edibles consisted of bottled water and cans of Spam. We should have bought some of that fried dough and ice cream at the arcade before our money had been magicked away.

At least this time I had no trouble finding the mail slot, which was what we had come back for. It was in the wall beneath the window, giving the appearance that any letters we wrote would drop directly into the empty flower box. Hopefully, even in the no-frills version of the game, there was mail pickup. Next to the slot was a little shelf that held several sheets of paper and a quill pen. These were not as fine as the parchment and the ostrich-plume pen from Emily's roll-top desk, but—as with the Spam—were better than nothing.

There was no place to sit. And there were no lamps. So I needed to work standing at the window, by the moonlight. Thank goodness for that full moon every night. I picked up the pen.

"Can't we rest just a little?" Emily begged from where she was sitting on one of the sleeping bags.

Don't whine, I wanted to snap at her. Instead, I told her, "You can rest while I compose the letter."

" 'kay," she said. "Grace?"

"What?"

Maybe I wasn't doing as great a job hiding my resentment as I thought, because she said, "I'm so sorry I got you into this."

"It's okay," I said, suddenly feeling that it was, in the face of her remorse. What kind of cold and insensitive sister was I? "I'm not leaving you, Emily."

"I won't hold you to that." She closed her eyes, letting her chin drop to her chest, not even taking the time to lie down.

This *had* to work.

I picked up the pen and wrote:

To the nearest dragon—
We've got gold.
Lots and lots of gold.
We bet you're not smart enough to get it from us.

Sincerely,
Grace and Emily Pizzelli

I reread the letter, then changed the last line:

The Pizzelli sisters: Grace and Emily

I don't know why I liked the sound of that better. More dramatic, I guess.

Emily was looking so peaceful, I decided not to bother her to get her opinion. The wording wasn't important. We needed to get a dragon ticked off enough that it would come to get our gold from us. Yeah, well, and if it wasn't completely ticked off before it came, it would be once it realized all we had were five gold pieces. But we'd have to deal with that later.

I folded the letter and dropped it into the mail slot. I listened carefully but didn't hear a thing. Which I guess was a hopeful sign. If it had really dropped into the flower box, that probably wouldn't have been a good thing.

When we'd had our tea party, our guests had rung the doorbell and servants had let them in. I very much doubted there was a doorbell, and there sure as heck weren't any servants in this house.

How long would it take? Before, the clock had already started chiming when I'd invited the girls to come at four o'clock, giving them like three seconds from the moment my fingers had let go of the letter to their arriving on our doorstep, dressed and ready to snarf down petits-fours.

Emily was snoring quietly, but I moved closer to the door so I could hear anyone approaching.

It's not that I expected the dragon to knock.

But neither was I expecting him to rip the roof off the house.

There I was listening for footsteps or the sound of beating wings. Instead, the nails holding the roof frame to the house squealed in protest.

There was a big difference between facing my sister transformed into a dragon and having this massive stranger-dragon perched on top of the open-to-the-sky wall of the house, holding the peeled-back roof in his claw, peeking at us like we were the last two wontons at the bottom of a box of Chinese takeout.

CHƎPƎER 21

Gold

W HEN MY SISTER had been a dragon—and how many people can say *that* with a straight face?—when my sister had been a dragon, she had still spoken with her normal human voice. When this dragon spoke, there was nothing normal or human about it. His voice was fire and gravel, ancient and relentless, the sound of tectonic plates grinding together before an earthquake.

"Give me the gold!" he demanded.

Whether it had been the ripping off of the roof or the geological voice of the dragon, Emily had awakened.

"Holy catastrophe, Batman," she said, "what have you gone and gotten us into?"

Maybe she was trying to be funny, but at that point if the dragon had told us "I require a human sacrifice," I would gladly have shoved her into his path.

The dragon's golden eyes didn't blink, but his forked tongue flicked, tasting the air. He repeated his demand, raising his already massive voice, as though we hadn't answered because we hadn't heard. "GIVE ME THE GOLD!"

Emily and I both dug into our pockets with shaking hands. We offered up our accumulated wealth: me, three coins; Emily, two. I didn't bother showing him the wooden nickels.

The dragon's tongue became more agitated, preparing us—okay, well, not really—for his roar: *"WHERE IS THE GOLD?"*

"This is it," I managed to squeak out.

The dragon bellowed, **"YOU SAID YOU HAD 'LOTS AND LOTS' OF GOLD."**

I looked at the coins in my hand and tried to sound sincere. *"I did?"*

Emily looked at me like *THIS is your plan? Oh, boy!*

The dragon retracted his snakelike tongue. That was the only warning we got before a stream of fire shot out of his mouth. Luckily, it wasn't aimed at us. But the partition blocking off the toilet went up in flames.

"You insulted me," the dragon growled, *"AND* **you have no gold?"**

"Sorry," I said. "Any way we can make it up to you?"

This was a kids' game, I reminded myself. I needed re-minding at that point. Regardless of what had happened, I was counting on there *not* being a human-flesh-eating dragon in a game that had been designed with glittery butterflies, unicorns, dolphins, and a flower-matching game. And that was about as far as the specifics of my plan went. So maybe Emily was right, and this catastrophe—this particular catastrophe—*was* my fault.

But maybe it wasn't a catastrophe after all.

The dragon puffed out his chest. (Yeah, like a dragon sitting on the corner of our house where he'd ripped off our roof had to make himself look bigger to be intimidating.) **"You will be my slaves,"** he announced.

"Okay," I said, and I was aware that Emily's eyebrows shot up.

Her expression said, *I don't know where you're going with this, Grace, so you're on your own.*

Actually, *slaves* sounded good. *Slaves* sounded like we would be serving him, and that was better than being served *to* him. "For how long?" I asked.

"Ninety-nine years."

Sure. Why not? That was as doable as King Rasmussem's eighty-seven-thousand-whatever gold pieces.

"When do we begin?" I asked.

"Now."

The dragon reached into the house and grabbed me in a taloned claw, his grip not tight enough to hurt, but tight enough that I couldn't fill my lungs for a good scream. Then he snatched Emily with his other claw. And then he threw himself into the night air.

His leathery wings beat noisily, something like when

you're standing directly beneath the huge school flag on a windy day. Something like that . . . times five.

Far below, even as we were still angling up, I glimpsed the lights of the Rasmussem arcade—the carousel, the midway, a Ferris wheel that was at the end of a path we'd never followed—and then there was the forest, miles and miles of forest. Occasionally, there were lights there, too, festively strung between trees, possibly marking a settlement. Once, our way briefly followed the course of a river, and between the snaps of the dragon's wings I could hear a few notes of ragtime music and I saw a brightly lit paddlewheel boat, a bejeweled miniature about as big as the palm of my hand.

By the light of the moon, I could see Emily hanging limply in the dragon's grasp. Fainted? Or fallen asleep? "Emily!" I shouted as loudly as my squeezed lungs would allow. But the wind caught my voice and flung it away.

If Emily . . . Damn! It was hard to bring myself to even think it. If Emily had died—not that she had, but *if* she had—would the dragon continue to carry her, or would he drop her?

I forced myself to believe that as insignificant as our weight was to him, he had no reason to carry her if she was dead and therefore useless to him. So she was still alive— she had to be, and that was *not* just wishful thinking on my part.

No.

Definitely not.

As eager as I was to believe, I still hadn't quite convinced myself by the time we came to the mountains.

The moon was behind us, so I could make out little detail. The dragon appeared to be flying full speed toward the face of a cliff.

I was too terrified to even close my eyes.

The dragon tilted sideways till he was almost entirely vertical, then he ducked his head and pulled his talons in closer to his body, which brought me in so that my face scraped against his scales. I hoped these were all good signs that he hadn't suddenly decided to commit suicide by mountain. Finally I saw the crack in the rock, and I just had time to think *It's too narrow!* when we were through it.

The dragon righted himself and landed with a soft sound like coins jangling in the bottom of a pocket.

No time for me to wonder *Where?* before he set me on my feet and breathed flame into the darkness. The clever dragon had torches in brackets lining the cave we'd entered, and all of those on the back wall ignited, throwing flickering light over us.

Some part of my brain registered that the cavern was at least as big as our school cafeteria, and that in the corner there were gold coins and artifacts piled high enough to make a decent sledding hill. But that wasn't the important thing. The important thing was that the dragon had set Emily on the floor, too, and I saw her move, curling herself into a more comfortable position. Another case of good news/bad news: bad that she could sleep through the terror of abduction by dragon, good that she was *only* sleeping.

I knelt beside her and shook her, but she didn't wake up. I took her hand in mine and squeezed. She may have squeezed back. Maybe. Or not. I brushed a couple strands of hair off her forehead, away from her eyes, but there definitely wasn't any reaction to that.

"I shall allow you to sleep now," the dragon informed us. His huge voice bounced around the cavern, threatening to cause a cave-in, or at the very least to give me a headache, but his words vindicated my belief that since this was a game for little kids, the dragon would not be as fierce as the kind my usual gaming brought me into contact with. **"There is an enchanted never-ending bucket of food to satisfy your hunger, and a toilet behind that big treasure chest."**

Typical. Rasmussem didn't want any little girl who ended up here to be deprived of necessities, and be traumatized, and not return to play another day. But I'd already used the facilities at Emily's house, and I'd had my fill of Spam. Still, my curiosity made me look at the enchanted bucket. KFC. Rasmussem must have gotten some serious product-placement considerations for that.

The dragon said, "Tomorrow, you will start polishing my gold. I want to be able to see my reflection in every single piece. The day after, you will polish my scales so that they shine as fully as the gold. The day after that, you will once again polish the gold. The day after that . . ."

This would be a boring ninety-nine years of service.

Not, of course, that either Emily or I had ninety-nine years.

Except, it suddenly occurred to me that *nobody* had ninety-nine years to spend keeping this dragon shiny. Most games play out over three to seven days in a half-hour of total immersion. Even one year waiting on this dragon would require at least fifty return trips to the Rasmussem arcade. No player would keep coming back that often just to buff and polish.

So there must be a way to escape.

All I had to do was figure out how.

And worry about the amount of time Emily had left.

Emily . . . I squeezed her hand again, and this time I *knew* there was no response. I wasn't sure if a good night's sleep would refresh my sister or if she would never awaken. What, exactly, did that score of twenty-two out of one hundred mean? That she had already spent more than three-fourths of the total time she had? She'd been here hours—which translated to days of game time—before I'd arrived. Surely almost 25 percent meant more than a few hours left. But that was assuming we were talking as though she were a car engine with a quarter of a tank of fuel left: one instant going, the next stopped. Or a time bomb ticking down from a hundred to zero: nothing . . . nothing . . . *kaboom!* As opposed to, for example, a person whose heart was working at 25 percent capacity. I'd seen that with both of my grandfathers. A wonky heart would cause all sorts of medical problems on top of diminished blood flow. Not being able to breathe, or having fluid accumulate, or getting a blood clot would kill such a patient before that last 1 percent closed off.

Thank you, King Rasmussem, for being as clear as mud.

Still, I remembered he had not considered lying and stealing to be cheating.

"Okay," I interrupted the dragon, who was still going on about the joys of shiny surfaces, "but what about the sprites?"

The dragon blinked, finally surprised by something I'd said. He told me, **"The sprites can polish their own gold."**

"That's not what I meant," I said. "I was wondering what protection you have against them."

The dragon's laughter bubbled out like magma.

"Protection? Against sprites? Itty-bitty smaller-than-YOU sprites?" His laughter caused a minor avalanche in the pile of gold.

"Who have magic," I reminded him.

"Who stole our gold," I lied to him.

The thought of stolen gold drained the humor out of him fast. While the dragon considered that, my mind continued to whirl with possibilities. If I could turn the dragon and the sprites against one another . . .

I added, "My sister and I had lots of gold."

"So you wrote," he grumbled at me.

"What?" I asked, as innocently as I could. "When? I never wrote to you. I don't even know your address."

"I came," the dragon said, annoyance beginning to seep through in his voice, **"because you said you had lots and lots of gold."**

"Oh," I said, as though understanding were dawning. "That's what you were talking about, back at Emily's house. No, I didn't write to you about our gold. Why would I? And you said something about insulting you?" I shook my head. "I didn't understand that part, either."

"YOU WROTE," the dragon bellowed, steam beginning to come out his ears, **"THAT YOU AND YOUR SISTER HAD LOTS AND LOTS OF GOLD, AND THAT I WASN'T SMART ENOUGH TO GET IT FROM YOU."**

"Ouch!" I said. "That wouldn't have been a very smart thing to say to you. Bragging about having gold? To a dragon? A big, powerful dragon like you?" Surely sucking up a bit couldn't hurt. "And then saying something mean to you on top of that? Why in the world would we ever do that?"

"*YOU* TELL *ME!*" the dragon insisted. "You're the ones who sent the letter. 'The Pizzelli sisters: Grace and Emily.' That's how you signed it. Do you deny that's who you are?"

"No," I said. "I just deny sending the letter." I was still holding Emily's hand, and I was concerned that all this roaring wasn't rousing her. *Please be all right, Emily.*

"IF NOT YOU," the dragon demanded, "*WHO?*"

"The sprites," I said. "I mean, they stole our gold, and we didn't have nearly as much as you."

The dragon looked thoughtful, as though he might believe me. It was time to escalate.

"The sprites have magical powers," I said. "And objects of magic. But that isn't enough for them. They put a spell on us, then came right in and took our gold. I couldn't move to stop them. I overheard them saying they want all the gold in the Land of the Golden Butterflies. Somehow or other, the spell wore off of me, but not my sister. That's why she won't wake up."

"Well, they won't be able to work their sprite magic on me," the dragon said.

"Maybe not," I said. "But what about your gold? They have the magic ability to change common things into gold— like the butterflies. But they also can change gold into common things. What if they do that to what you have here?"

"What do you mean?" the dragon asked.

Which was my cue for the next part of my plan.

"Oh, no!" I cried. I ran forward and pretended to pick up one of the gold coins from his horde. But what I held out to show him was one of the wooden nickels King Rasmussem had given me. "It's already started."

CHAPTER 22

Spriteville

T HE DRAGON'S WINGS shot out and he was instantly airborne and flapping his way toward the exit.

"No!" I cried. "Wait!"

I was calling the dragon back.

What a brilliant tactician! Obviously, I needed a remedial course in fantasy gaming if the best plan I could come up with had me unwilling to part company with a dragon who had already declared his intention to have me spend my next ninety-nine years polishing every surface in the cave.

But while having him fly away to wage war on the sprites led to delightful mental images, it wouldn't help Emily and me. I doubted that King Rasmussem would cancel our so-called debt to the sprites if sprites ceased to exist on account of the dragon's incinerating every last one of them. Also, I had to admit there was an equal possibility that the sprites might incinerate the dragon. They were just mean enough that I couldn't put dragon-conquering beyond them. Then here I'd be, stuck in this mile-high cave, waiting for our time to run out, with Emily sound asleep through it all.

And the only thing that could make *that* possibility even worse was if the sprites learned who had set the dragon on them.

The dragon hovered, not quite like a hummingbird, because his wings weren't beating nearly fast enough to keep him aloft in a world without magic. **"What?"** he demanded.

"You'd better take us with you," I told him. "You're too . . ." Years of experience in the real world, especially as a girl, had ingrained in me that *big* was a negative word. ". . . grand . . ." That wasn't quite right. ". . . imposing . . ." What *was* the word I was looking for?

"Big?" the dragon supplied.

"Noticeable," I countered.

"Big comes in useful for stepping on a bunch of sprites all at once," the dragon said.

"Well, yes," I said. "But not so much for finding their magic . . ." Magic what? ". . . um, magic well—the one that changes stuff like this"—I held up the wooden nickel—"to gold. And that changes gold—"

"Yeah, yeah," he interrupted, **"to stuff like that. I got it."**

I shook my head. "No, de-golding"—*Is* there such a word? Never mind, he knew what I meant—"is a slow-acting spell, because the sprites like to gloat while the gold owners get frenzied as they see what's happening but are unable to do anything to stop it. What the sprites' magic well does"—okay, I'd said *well*, so I needed to stick with it—"is change gold into more gold."

"More gold?" That was an idea clearly close to his heart. **"What are you saying?"** The dragon stopped hovering, which was good because it was disconcerting, being so against the laws of physics and all. Not that it wasn't disconcerting to have him settle to the ground right in front of—and towering over—me.

I said, "Toss in one coin, get two back."

He narrowed his eyes suspiciously. **"How does that work?"**

"I don't understand magic," I protested, playing dumb—not that big a stretch. "How does your never-ending bucket of fried chicken work?"

The dragon considered. And seemed to buy it. Still . . . **"And you would help me,"** he asked, **"on account of the long-standing friendship between us?"**

"On account of," I corrected him, "my enmity with the sprites. I would help anyone if it got back at them."

His taloned claw shot out and took hold of me. He didn't believe me and was about to squeeze the life out of me, I was sure of it.

But then I realized that he was in the air and we were out of the cave.

Without Emily.

Without Emily.

"What are you doing?" I screamed at him.

"Flying to the island of the sprites," he told me in his big, booming voice, **"to get their magic well from them."**

"You can't do that!" I yelled.

Did he hear me? He had to hear me, but he didn't respond.

Maybe he thought I was talking from a moralistic standpoint. Or that I doubted his strength.

I knew "because you can't abandon my sister" wouldn't be a winning argument.

I told him, "A well doesn't work if it's out of the ground." Of course, we were talking about a magic well, so was that the same? Oh, wait a sec. *I was making the whole thing up.* All I had to do was sound reasonable enough to convince the dragon. "A well—any well—draws its strength from the ground. Uproot it, and all you'll have is a lawn decoration."

The dragon's speed had decreased noticeably.

"What you need to do—" I started.

"—is kill off all the sprites," he interrupted, **"so I can use the well where it is."**

As engaging as that thought was, I'd already calculated that it wouldn't help. "Yes," I said. "Except . . . it's hard to say if the sprites' magic would die with them."

Annoyed—probably at my constantly saying he was wrong—the dragon blew a tongue of flame into the night air.

"I have a suggestion," I told him.

Since he didn't throw me down to the earth in exasperation, I continued, speaking in fits and starts as the words came to me, urging him to move quickly, because I didn't want him to have enough time to think about the implausibility of all this.

"What you should do—and I'll help you, since the sprites have been so mean to me and my sister—is bring a whole bunch of your gold—quickly, before it turns bad—to their land, and double it—because magically created gold can't be . . ."—I still didn't have a word for it—". . . de-golded—so you'll be safe from their wily schemes. If we work quietly and secretly, they won't know what we're up to, and you can make several batches of tamper-free gold."

I saw he was heading toward a mountain. He had stopped believing me, and was about to hurl me at its side. Closer . . . closer . . .

There was a crack in the stone. Maybe he'd flung other annoying people at the same place . . .

Oh, no, wait. It was *his* mountain. I'd been too caught up in trying to get him to turn back to realize that he had circled around.

Through that narrow entry he shot, skidding to a stop

beyond where Emily still lay snoozing, and he dropped me onto the pile of gold.

Ouch! Don't believe what people say about gold being a "soft" metal.

"There's a flying carpet," the dragon told me. **"Somewhere beneath that."**

After some digging—after quite a bit of digging—we found it, rolled up in a corner.

Not that I've ever seen a flying carpet before, but I'd assumed it would look like an Oriental rug—you know, deep burgundy or midnight-blue, lots of flowers or geometric shapes, an intricate design that desert nomad women had spent years weaving from traditional motifs. This looked like the pink shaggy rug my aunt Kathy has in her guest bathroom. Except bigger. A little bigger. I'm estimating probably three people could sit on it.

The dragon started piling gold on the rug, from edge to edge, to edge to edge—and about as high up as someone sitting. I have no idea what gold was worth on the current exchange, but this looked to be at least ten times the amount Emily had kept in her treasure chest in the pavilion, so I strongly suspected our almost-eighty-eight-thousand-gold-piece fine would be covered.

"Carpet, up," the dragon commanded. **"Follow, and do not lose your cargo."**

The carpet rose off the ground.

This time, I was waiting and watching for the dragon's claw to come at me. "Wait!" I cried.

"NOW WHAT?" he thundered.

"My sister. We can't leave her behind."

"Of course we can," he said, picking me up and flying through the crack, back out into the world.

I craned around and saw the carpet tip to fit sideways, and not a single coin fell.

"It costs you nothing to bring my sister!" I screamed over the sound of the wind and the flapping of the dragon's wings. "And you keep my goodwill."

"I'll keep more of your goodwill," the dragon said, "if you are dependent on me to see your sister again."

Okay, so maybe he wasn't as gullible as I'd hoped.

The mountain grew smaller and smaller with each powerful beat of the dragon's wings. And then it was lost in the distance and the darkness of night.

Emily! I'm sorry!

I tried to send my thoughts zinging telepathically to my sister.

Not that there was any reason to believe telepathy worked in this world.

But I had promised I'd stay with her.

Of course, there was no real reason to believe she knew or felt anything anymore. She had slept through all the dragon's earthquake-sized roars, and there was no evidence she would have somehow been aware if I'd been sitting by her side. She didn't know I'd abandoned her.

Still, *I* did.

It was probably all for the best that the last thing Emily had been conscious of was that I was working on a plan, and that she didn't know it had failed.

I stopped looking behind us, where all I could see was the flying carpet keeping up with us, and turned in the direction the dragon was flying. There was a glow coming over the horizon. *It can't be dawn*, I thought. Surely it wasn't that late. Besides, this didn't look like dawn. I associated sunrise with pink and mauve and orange, and clouds outlined in light almost too bright to look at.

And this was just white glow.

More like, I realized, light pollution.

We were approaching a big city.

We were flying over water, coming on an island. The dragon had said the sprites lived on an island. But I had pictured meadows and streams and toadstool houses or darling little nestlike homes built into trees, maybe a tiny Dutch-style windmill or two.

Instead, there were skyscrapers. Okay, they were sprite-sized skyscrapers, which means they looked more like Barbie Does Manhattan than like New York or Tokyo. But since we were in the air, that just made me feel as though I were in an airplane, high above a metropolitan center. Some bored designer at Rasmussem obviously had an untraditional sense of humor and way too much time on his hands, designing something so elaborate that 99 percent of players would never see.

As the dragon lowered, coming in for a landing, we could see sprite-sized sports cars and stretch limos. On the street corners, FLUTTER and DON'T FLUTTER traffic signals guided the pedestrians. Electronic billboards and neon lights announced stores and casinos, live entertainment, hair-relaxing treatments, and—who could have guessed?—karaoke bars. As we got even nearer, I could hear a tiny little voice singing "Achy-Breaky Heart." So far, nobody had looked up and noticed us blotting out the stars, but that wouldn't last long.

"Where is this magic well?" the dragon demanded.

I'd been expecting to be able to tell the dragon he needed to wait for me on the outskirts of the sprites' settlement. I'd thought I could offer to sneak the gold to the well, but that instead I would find a sprite or two on whom to bestow the gold on behalf of all spritekind, and that this act would send me and Emily back home before the dragon realized I'd betrayed him. But there were no outskirts.

Another plan fallen flat on its face.

"Where is this magic well?" the dragon repeated. A complication evidently crossed his dragon mind. **"How will you know it when you see it?"**

Good question.

I had no answer.

Somebody had spotted us. Sprites were beginning to point up at us, their shrill voices complaining.

And then I saw it—a pair of water fountains in front of a building that had signs in the windows flashing LOTTO and SHOES—EXTRA-WIDE SIZES. The sprays of water from the fountains were illuminated by changing colored lights and were timed to spritz into each other, forming a watery arch for customers entering the establishment to walk under.

And that, I figured, was the closest thing to a magic well I was going to find here.

"There!" I shouted to the dragon, pointing.

"Which one is the magical one?"

He was the only one for whom it made a difference. "The one on the right," I assured him.

"IF YOU ARE DECEIVING ME, YOU WILL SUF-FER," the dragon warned.

Didn't I know that already?

"Carpet!" the dragon commanded. **"Into the water!"**

The carpet hurtled downward. It was big enough, and heavy enough, and traveling at a great enough speed that when it splashed into the fountain, the ensuing wall of water drenched all the sprites on that city block.

Ooo, and I thought they'd been shrill and complaining before.

Before the dragon could notice that all we had was wet, angry sprites, not twice as much gold, I shouted down at them: "A gift from Grace and Emily Pizzelli—a repayment of our debt to you, as directed by King Rasmussem!"

Except they didn't say, "Oh, well, then, that's that, thank you very much." And King Rasmussem didn't materialize and say, "Good job, so I'll send you both back home now." And there was no fizziness and returning to Rasmussem.

It hadn't worked.

My plan hadn't worked.

"WHAT TRICKERY IS THIS?" the dragon roared. He shook me until my brain rattled. Even after he stopped with the shaking, no doubt preferring a still target for when he blasted his dragon breath at me, I couldn't see straight, and my brain continued bouncing off the sides of my skull, making a disconcerting *click click click click click* sound.

It's alarming to hear your brain clatter around inside your head.

Except it's sort of, I realized, wondering what was taking the dragon so long to finish me off, *it's kind of like King Rasmussem's arcade wheel*—the one that showed how much life force Emily and I had left.

But not really, because it was more like a hospital's heart monitor.

And then I heard Ms. Bennett say, "She's back."

CHAPTER 23

Playing by the Numbers

IT WAS PROBABLY because I'd been hearing that heart monitor that I had the impression my heart must have stopped and a doctor back at Rasmussem had started to pound my chest.

But then I realized, no, it was just that Mom had thrown herself across me. "Grace!" she cried, her voice muffled against my T-shirt. "Grace! Thank God!"

And it was that, more than Ms. Bennett's words, "*She's back*," that told me Emily wasn't with me.

It's not that I'm mentally whining, *Mom and Dad always loved Emily best*. But Emily had been gone longer, much longer, and I had to believe that if we'd both returned to Rasmussem, Mom was more likely to acknowledge her first.

"I'm all right," I said, struggling to sit up, to see Emily, even though I knew there was nothing new to see.

Ms. Bennett was in the cubicle, as was Adam, the tech guy. I'd been expecting to see my father, summoned back from California after all this time. But then I realized that, although I'd been away two days in the game, that meant no more than a half hour had passed in the real world. Most likely, Dad was still in his meeting and didn't even know about Emily yet.

I could see Emily on the other couch, motionless. She was the one with the heart monitor attached to her. That was new. Someone at Rasmassem was worried that her condition was deteriorating. *Beep . . . beep . . . beep . . .* Steady. No sign of stress. No sign of waking up. I'd hoped that, maybe, she was right behind me.

Apparently not.

Apparently, the king of the gypsies wasn't going to accept money returned to the sprites on behalf of Emily if Emily wasn't present.

It's not fair! I wanted to shout. *She would have been with me if that stupid dragon hadn't been so stubborn!*

Instead, I said, "Okay, I've got it now. Send me back."

"Are you out of your mind?" my mother demanded.

Well, maybe, but that wasn't what was important.

"It's all set now," I said. "I understand why the *Return Home* function wasn't working, and it's working again."

Ms. Bennett looked skeptical, and that was worse than Mom not believing. "I don't know—" she started.

"There's no time!" I shouted. "I know how to get Emily!"

Mom's fingers were digging into my shoulders. She

shook me and shouted right back at me, "I can't lose both of you!" Her voice was ragged, her eyes red, the area between her nose and her lip slick with snot, evidence that she had spent most of the last thirty minutes sobbing, too distressed to worry about appearances. "I can't lose both of you," she said more calmly, to impress on me that she meant it.

"You don't need to lose either one of us," I assured her. Assured Ms. Bennett. Assured Adam, although I doubt he really cared all that much. "I need, like, three minutes, tops," I told them. "I can do this."

"Grace . . ." Mom said in a tone that I knew meant no.

"Mom, she was afraid to come home because she thought you and Dad would be angry and disappointed in her. But now she knows that *disappointed* is better than *devastated*. She's changed her mind. She wants to come back. All I need to do is fetch the magic carpet, return to the cave, hope the dragon isn't there yet, get Emily, pile on more gold, and talk the sprites into accepting it."

Mom squinted, trying to concentrate, trying to follow this.

"Never mind," I said. "The point is I know how to do it, but time is running out."

"What if something else goes wrong," Mom asked, "and you get stuck in there again?"

"What if I get run over by a car while I'm on my way to school?" I countered. "What if a plane crashes into our house? You can't protect me against everything, and I can't live life afraid to move."

"Not the same," Mom said.

"I can do this," I repeated.

Mom bit her lip. "Or do you just really, really want to believe you can?"

I hoped it wasn't only wishful thinking, although I knew it might be. I simply said, once more, "I can do it."

She was crying again, her whole body shaking, but since she wasn't actually saying no, I acted as though she'd given permission. I hugged her and said, "Five minutes at the very most. Count to five hundred. Before you get there, I'll be back. Emily and I will be back." It was so hard to look at her in this much pain that I turned away to Ms. Bennett to tell her, "Don't put me with Emily. Put me where the magic carpet is."

She was biting her lip, too, but then she reached over to the console, and I quickly lay down.

I heard Adam whisper to her in a warning singsong, "Mr. Kroll isn't going to like this," and I closed my eyes to pretend that I was already there, that it was already too late for any of us to change her mind.

A butterfly landed on my arm, welcoming me back to the Land of the Golden Butterflies. But I was lying on something cold and wet and lumpy and—Oh! What was that stench?

I opened my eyes and saw that my nose was inches away from a broken laundry basket full of old, crunched-down-heel sneakers. Both the laundry basket and the shoes were sprite-sized. Eww! Who would have thought such pretty little creatures had such stinky feet?

During the three or four minutes I'd spent at Rasmussem, time here had continued, and the sun had come up, casting an early-morning golden glow on my surroundings. One thing was certain: although I was outside, I was no longer in the city in front of the pair of water fountains.

But where *was* I?

I sat up. Beyond the split laundry basket was a rusted doll-sized shopping cart that was minus one wheel and had one smashed-in corner. The cart held a shadeless table lamp, a tarnished wall mirror, and a wall clock with a cracked face and only one hand. And beyond that were bundled-up-and-tied-with-a-string newspapers and magazines and books piled on an ugly couch that had no cushions. And beyond that, a chipped and dented washing machine had been placed on the roof of a sprite limo that had no doors, no seat, and no engine. And beyond that . . .

What a bunch of junk! I thought.

And with that, I finally put together where I was: a junkyard.

Acres and acres of junkyard.

Wonderful. How would I ever find the magic carpet in all this garbage?

I stood up and found the carpet. That was the cold, wet, lumpy thing I'd been lying on. Apparently, someone had fished it out of the fountain and not realized it was worth drying and saving.

Although now I was chilled and stiff, not to mention wearing soggy clothing, this, finally, was a little bit of luck. I was overdue for luck.

"Carpet," I ordered, "up."

Nothing. Could dampness have caused it to experience the magical equivalent of shorting out?

I was trying to wring it like a bulky, cold, nasty washcloth, when a voice like a landslide bellowed, **"I knew I shouldn't have trusted you!"**

Dropping the rug, I whirled around.

It was the dragon. Of course it was the dragon.

I took a step back. Not that a step back was going to save me from a blast of his fiery breath. Nor would it keep him from grabbing hold of me and squeezing the life out of me with his powerful claw. Or finishing that shake-my-brain-loose action my return to Rasmussem had interrupted. Or how about popping me into his mouth like a salted peanut?

But the fact that I had the time to think up these dire alternatives proved . . . well, I'm not sure what it proved, but it proved something.

I took a closer look at the dragon.

He wasn't shiny as he'd appeared the night before, as though being in this junkyard had dulled and bedraggled him. He was as big as ever, but he was . . . I don't know . . . Can a dragon droop? He was slouching, as if he was tired. Or—I suddenly realized—depressed. That could well have been because he had a chain around his neck. Like a dog's choke collar. A longer chain hung from the collar: a leash that wound around the piles of ruined cars and discarded furniture and leaky bags of garbage, and must have had its other end fastened to something to keep him from wandering.

Instead of running, instead of saying, "End game . . . ," instead of any other reasonable response, I asked, "What happened?"

"Captured by the sprites," the dragon said, his voice as diminished as his stature, no more than distant thunder. **"Forced to . . ."** He sighed, and the hem of my dress started to smoke from the spark that escaped his lips, but I could tell it was unintentional. I beat at my skirt to keep it from igniting while the dragon finished, **". . . guard this place."** Another sigh, this one flameless. **"I am reduced to being a junkyard dog."**

"I am so sorry," I said. And I really was. I mean, for someone who loved gold and shiny things, this had to be especially hard.

"Ah, well," he said, **"the only good thing is that the**

terms of my imprisonment aren't long." Before I could say, *Well, at least there's that,* he finished, **"Only ninety-nine years."**

Which just goes to show the difference between dragons and humans.

"Still," I said, "I *am* sorry. But I was desperate to rescue my sister."

"I understand," the sagging dragon assured me. He explained, **"I, too, had a sister, once."**

The past tense didn't escape me. "What happened to her?" I asked, feeling we were connected, two of a kind after all, sharing similar personal tragedies.

"I had to eat her," the dragon said, **"to keep her from stealing my gold."**

Which, I guess, points to an even bigger difference between dragons and humans.

"Listen," I said, "*my* sister still needs rescuing. If you help me, I'll help you."

A little bit of the glint came back into the dragon's eyes, and I was glad he was at the farthest extent of his leash. I still took a couple of steps back, even as the dragon told me, **"Been there, done that."**

"I need to return to your cave to fetch my sister," I explained. "Plus, I need eighty-eight thousand gold coins."

"At least you're being up-front about it this time," the dragon said.

"I'd planned to use the magic carpet, but it doesn't seem to be working."

The dragon gave me a long, level look. **"The carpet is mine. That is why it does not obey your command."**

"Well, then," I said, "will you give me the carpet, too, if I release you?"

"*Eighty-eight thousand* pieces of gold?" the dragon asked, in a tone that indicated the very thought was painful—in a tone that, in fact, indicated I might be following in the footsteps of his sister.

"It's not doing you any good while you're here," I pointed out. And because I knew *more* was always *better* with this dragon and his gold, I added, "And if I let you go, maybe you can get some of it back from the sprites."

The dragon thought this over, then said, **"You'll understand, of course, when I say release me first, and THEN I'll give you the carpet and the gold."**

"Promise?"

The dragon sighed, this time remembering to turn his head away from me. **"Promise."**

"All right, what do we have here?" I said as the dragon settled himself down to bring the choke collar within my reach.

"Combination lock," he said, though by then I could see. **"Three numbers: Left, right, then left again."**

"And the numbers?"

The dragon shook his head.

Of course he didn't know the numbers.

Which was a shame, because this lock went from 1 all the way to 100. Emily, being the math genius sister, probably knew a formula to figure out how many possible variations of a 3-number combination you could make with 100 numbers, but I was just as well satisfied to think, *Too many.* The good thing was that in games, they don't count on you just randomly trying every possible combination.

"Okay," I said, "the numbers have to be significant somehow. Are there any numbers around here?"

The dragon shrugged. **"Not that I've seen."**

"Does this place have a street address? Or an established-on date? A poster with an in-case-of-emergency phone number?"

"Don't know."

Maybe I needed to count the number of links on his chain leash . . . but I could easily see that there were more than one hundred links, and besides, it was dragging through some pretty yucky stuff, so I convinced myself, *Probably not.*

The dial was set at 1, so I spun it over 100 to 99, since 99 was the length of the dragon's sentence. I put my ear to the lock, like safecrackers do in the movies, and heard a very faint *click.* Great! I turned the dial to the right. *Click!* That was a surprise. What were the chances that I had figured out the first number and accidentally found the second: 99 and 100? I turned to the left. Once more it clicked at 99. But the lock didn't release. I turned to 100 again. *Click.* I spun the dial. 1: *Click.* 2: *Click.* 3: *Click.* Okay, it clicked with every single number. Still I listened carefully as I turned the dial from 1 to 100, hoping to hear something a little different, to feel something. But no. Evidently, I'd have to get all three numbers right before anything happened.

"I hate this," I muttered.

The dragon shrugged.

I used the numbers from my birthday. From Emily's birthday. From the dragon's birthday. Nothing.

What numbers were significant in this game?

There weren't any, I told myself. The only numbers . . . the only numbers . . .

I turned the dial quickly to hear the tiny *click click click click.*

The only numbers of real significance had been the ones on the gypsy king's wheel.

I reset the lock. Then turned left to 100, which was the optimum score, the one the game characters or someone just entering the game had. Turned right to the number the wheel had landed on for me: 87. Turned left to go to Emily's score of 22.

But luckily, I was turning very slowly.

And listening.

I heard a distinct *click!* before I got to 22, when I hit 9.

The lock released.

100-87-9.

Yay!

Except . . .

I sucked in a breath as I realized that 9 must be what Emily's level had fallen to.

While I was working on not panicking, the dragon wriggled out of the collar. He instantly stood taller, and his scales regained some of their luster. **"Thank you,"** he rumbled at me. **"Be quick, before I change my mind."** To the waterlogged wad of pink shag rug, the dragon said, **"I give you to Grace Pizzelli. Obey her as you would me."**

The little rug just lay there.

I looked at the dragon and held my hands out, as in, *Well?*

He mimicked my gesture.

Which must mean, I figured, that the answer was obvious.

So I said the obvious: "Carpet, up."

The carpet rose, a bit unsteadily, I thought, and hung in the air at about my chest level, dripping water. I was about to say, "Carpet, wring yourself," when it shook itself off like a wet dog.

"Aw, geez!" I said, wiping the splatters off myself. At least—at the *very* least—it wouldn't feel as though I were sitting in a puddle. "Carpet, down."

The carpet went down so that I could sit on it. "Thank you," I said to the dragon.

"**Hmph!**" he said.

"Carpet," I commanded, "to the dragon's cave."

CHAPTER 24

Going Back to *Where?*

RIDING BY MAGIC CARPET is smoother than being carried by dragon. In case that question ever comes up.

The little area rug, now that it was dry, now that it was in the air, was thick and soft and comfortable. It didn't flap, just soared, steady and noiseless.

Over the water we went, and over the forest. I guess I'd become blasé as a magical frequent-flyer, and after a short while I lay down rather than sit, remembering to repeat the dragon's order: "Do not lose your cargo."

I put my head on my arms and didn't exactly nap but rested. The carpet hadn't picked up any bad smells from having been soaked and spending the night in a garbage heap. Instead, there was a scent somewhere between vanilla and incense.

The sun was pleasantly warm on my back, drying the fabric of my once-white dress, and the front edge of the carpet curved inward, acting to deflect the air up and over me, so all I felt was a gentle breeze, no tearing wind.

Peaceful and relaxing, it reminded me of drifting on the float in Aunt Kathy's pool. Without the possibility of obnoxious cousin Brandon making rude comments.

Occasionally, I would open my eyes a crack to watch the world pass beneath me . . .

. . . until one time I opened my eyes and saw the world tipped over on its side.

"Do not lose your cargo! Do not lose your cargo!" I screamed at the carpet, digging my fingers into the nap of the rug, though I did not have the sensation of sliding off.

But the carpet clearly remembered it wasn't supposed to lose its cargo. It wasn't tilting on its side to dump me, it was hurtling through the vertical crevice that led into the dragon's cave.

The carpet slid to a gentle stop right beside Emily, who opened one eye, mumbled, "I'm up, I'm up," then went back to sleep. The look of her skin (gray and waxy) and the sound of her breathing (loud and wheezy) had me worried.

"Emily, I have a plan!" I told her, forcing enthusiasm into my voice. "And this one's a good one!"

Okay, well, I'd tell her again once she was awake. And I'd let her sleep, conserve her strength, until it was time to go.

Meanwhile, I threw handful after handful of gold onto the carpet.

"Almost there," I told Emily—well, actually, told myself. "You can kiss this world goodbye."

Except, now that I had the carpet loaded, where would Emily and I fit?

On top, I guess. Though lying on top of a heap of gold would be more stylish but less comfortable than lying on a plush bathroom carpet.

Still . . . "Emily." I shook my sister hard. "Emily."

She managed to get her eyes open. "'Lo, Grace," she said.

"Stand up," I ordered.

She groaned and shook her head.

"Stand up," I repeated. "You need to walk about five steps, then take one big step up, then you can lie down again, and we'll be home in no time."

"'kay," she said, but didn't move.

I took hold of her shoulders and dragged her to the carpet. She neither helped nor hindered me. "There," I said. "Forget the five steps; all you need to do is the one big step up."

From behind me came a familiar flapping noise I couldn't for the moment place; then the cave dimmed as something blocked the sunlight from outside.

Something big.

Something that took up just about all the space of that narrow entry into the cave.

Then a voice like a continent settling into place told me, **"I'm sorry. I can't do it. I can't let you take my gold. I've changed my mind."**

No! That was the game going just too far!

"You promised!" I snarled—or maybe I whined—at the dragon, sounding, by my own estimation, about five years old.

"Sorry," the dragon repeated.

Hard to gauge the sincerity of a creature who's big enough to step on you, except by noting the fact that he's *not* choosing to step on you.

"But I helped you," I reminded him. "I rescued you from ninety-nine years of junkyard dog duty."

"And I didn't eat you," the dragon pointed out, logic it was hard to find fault with. **"Carpet,"** he commanded, **"put the gold down."**

The carpet didn't budge.

The dragon told it, **"Carpet, I take back my giving you to Grace Pizzelli."**

Still nothing. It seemed the carpet didn't do take-backs.

As though he thought I wasn't the kind of person to hold a grudge, the dragon told me, **"I didn't eat you, AND I gave you my magic carpet."**

"Liar! Cheater!"

Taking his cue from the gypsy king, he said, **"It's just good gamesmanship."** Then, sounding considerably less friendly, he added, **"Now unload the gold before I change my mind about letting you and your sister go."**

Sullenly, I gave the carpet the order, "Carpet, dump the gold."

The clever carpet, catching my mood, flipped, and sent the gold crashing to the cave floor.

"My gold better not be dinged or dented," the dragon grumbled.

While he stepped forward to examine the spilled treasure, I saw that Emily's eyes were open. Open and enormous. Apparently, this early in a new day, after having slept most of yesterday, she had the strength to be awakened, if not by an urgent sister, at least by a miffed dragon.

Quietly, I motioned for her to get onto the carpet. I figured quiet was good. We didn't need to draw the dragon's attention to us, now that his gold was off our carpet and safely where he wanted it on his cavern floor.

Emily crawled onto the carpet. I'm not the one who can judge whether she didn't have the strength to stand or if that was a stealth move.

I sat behind her so that I could hold on to her, and I did my best to ignore how I could feel the heat of Emily's skin through our clothes. She definitely had a fever. I whispered, "Carpet, up, and out of here." I hurriedly added, "And don't lose your cargo."

Emily's fingers dug into my arm, and she didn't loosen her grip, even after the carpet straightened from flying out of the dragon's cave and into the morning light. "You have a knack for complicated plans I don't understand," she told me.

"That *wasn't* my plan," I told her.

"You said you had a plan, a good one."

She'd picked a fine time to be listening.

"Yeah," I snapped, "but that wasn't it."

"Off plan. Off plan," Emily said. I'm guessing she was trying to mimic the slightly mechanical voice that our car's GPS uses to tell us we're off route, but her voice was a ragged whisper. "Take your first safe opportunity to make a U-turn."

The fact that Emily—in her state—was trying to use humor to make me feel better *did* make me feel better. But it made me feel worse at the same time. And, wow, did I ever wish we could U-turn right out of this hateful game.

But speaking of directions, I realized that we weren't heading in one; we were just hovering about a carpet-length or so from the cave's entrance, because all I'd told the carpet was to get out of there. This was not a safe place to be, relative to a dragon with a track record of changing his mind.

I considered our options. Returning to Emily's home was pointless—there was nothing there for us, not even a roof. We could go back to the arcade, where I could try to convince the gypsy king to rethink his sentence on us. I could argue that of course it counted for me to have returned the sprites' gold on Emily's behalf . . . Yeah, like that was going to get us anywhere.

I told the carpet, "Take us once more to the island of the sprites."

"Sprites?" Emily asked as the carpet started moving. "But we don't have any gold to give them."

"I'm working on that part of the plan," I told her.

"Okay," she said. She leaned back against me, which I worried was a sign that she was making herself comfortable for going back to sleep, which was bad news, two and a half minutes after waking up.

But she didn't fall asleep right away. She said, "I'm sure you'll come up with something. You're so good at this. You always have great ideas."

It was hard to believe my ears. "I'm terrible at this," I argued. "My ideas stink."

"No," she said. Her voice was trembling. *She* was trembling. All she had was nine miserable points, and that was falling fast.

I told her, "You shouldn't be talking. Save your strength."

"No," she repeated more forcefully, "I need to say this."

I figured it was best not to put her in a position where she felt she had to argue, so I didn't interrupt again.

She said, "You're smart, and you're brave, and you're resourceful, and I am so proud to be your sister." She tightened her arms around my arms, the best she could do to hug me, given my position behind her.

In my smart, brave, resourceful way—I burst into tears.

"It's okay, Grace," she assured me, her voice little more

than a sigh in my ear. "Whatever happens, it's okay. I love you, and I know I can never repay all you've done for me."

This was pretty heady stuff for someone who'd always thought of herself as the "un-" sister, the one who wasn't pretty, or smart, or popular, the one whose own father couldn't come up with anything more exciting to praise her for than being levelheaded—which had always struck me as a scraping-the-bottom-of-the-barrel compliment. But it suddenly occurred to me that it wasn't. Okay, so, levelheaded, steady. Yeah, just like the tortoise who won the race. So what if that's not the most glamorous comparison in the world?

It's not the worst thing to be, either.

Emily said, "I wish I could be as quick-witted as you, as able to think on my feet. *You* don't need to cheat, because you never give up."

Well, once she said that, I had to come up with a new plan.

And Emily even stayed awake long enough for me to coach her on what to say, while I basked in the glow of me and my sister, together.

The morning had not progressed much beyond *early* when we arrived at the city of the sprites.

Emily was slumped against me, once more asleep, her breathing loud and labored, reminiscent of my grandfather's when he was in hospice. I had the carpet swing down to a new building that was going up, where four sprite construction workers with tiny little lunch pails and orange hardhats were too busy sitting on a beam and whistling at passersby to notice us hovering beside them at their fifth-floor level. I got to deliver the classic line from those cheesy sci-fi movies that are sometimes rerun between infomercials: "Take me to your leader."

It's a good thing they were sprites, because one was so startled he fell off the beam. But he fluttered right back up to the others, one of whom responded—very cleverly, I might point out—"What?" Then, unable to leave it at that, he added, "Grubby human girl."

I ignored the jibe, which was, after all, 100 percent accurate. "Your leader," I repeated. To their smirky little faces I suggested, "King? Queen? President? Prime minister? Governor? Mayor?" I was running out of steam. "General? Chief? CEO? Supervisor? Principal? Spokesperson?"

Finally, one of them took pity on me. "Brains-in-your-butt girl, we don't have any of those."

I asked, "Who makes the laws?"

"Annoying twit of a human," he called me, "we pretty much do what we want to do."

Why didn't that come as a surprise?

"Okay, well . . ." I gave Emily a shake. "Wake up," I told her.

"I'm up," she mumbled.

"Sprites are here," I said, hoping she'd remember her lines. "Tell them what you wanted to tell them."

She patted my leg and told the sprites, "This is the best sister, ever," which was *not* what I'd instructed her to say.

"Thank you," I said, ignoring the sprites' finger-down-the-throat gagging gestures. "But I meant what you came here to say."

She was wobbly, like her head was too heavy.

"About the gold . . ." I prompted.

That one word made the sprites knock off their foolishness.

"Gold," Emily repeated. "We've got gold for you."

Close enough.

And a good thing, because her chin dropped to her chest and she began snoring.

I finished for her, "King Rasmussem—the gypsy king?—he told us we owed you money, and we've gathered it in a cave to the north. You guys willing to act as representatives and accept it on behalf of all spritekind?"

They were all bobbing their heads and saying things like "Well, sure, pretty girl," and "Of course, lovely lass," and "*We* can distribute the gold for you, clever youngster."

Yeah, like that's going to happen, I thought, but I hid my skepticism. The king had said we needed to give the money to the sprites. He hadn't actually specified to *all* the sprites, so I hoped four construction workers would count. "Great," I said. "Climb aboard, or follow me. Your choice."

The construction workers put their little heads to-gether; then one of them said, "Faster if we magically trans-port there. A bright young thing like you can readily see that."

This had to be one for the record books: sprites offer-ing to *donate* a magic spell.

"I don't know how to describe where it is," I told them. Not to mention that I didn't trust them one pixie inch. Since I was already fudging with the number of sprites, I didn't want to risk that *sending* them to the gold was as good as *giving* them the gold.

We compromised by having them transport us to the northern mountains, saving us *some* time. As the sprites flut-tered in a cluster alongside us, I whispered, just loudly enough for the carpet to hear, "Take us to—but not into—the dragon's cave. And when we're about thirty seconds out, give a little bob to let me know."

I hoped thirty seconds would be long enough to get Emily coherent again.

We had flown for less than a minute when the carpet either bobbed or hit a speed bump. I couldn't see the dis-tinctive crack that was the entryway, but I had a tendency to miss it till the last couple of seconds anyway. What if I was wrong, and we'd simply been jostled by an aberration of a wind current?

Sometimes you just need to trust your magic carpet. I pinched Emily.

"Ow!" she said crankily. I think she said. It was hard to tell with all the rasping and wheezing.

"Behold the gold . . ." I prompted.

She was trying to find a comfortable position, and groggily and grumpily asked, "What gold?"

"Behold the gold . . ." I repeated.

Wasn't that the crack that marked the cave up ahead?

It was, I determined, just as Emily caught on and managed to squeak out, "Behold the gold."

But I interrupted, commanding between clenched teeth, "Louder."

"Behold the gold," Emily declared, even managing a theatrical wave in the general vicinity ahead of us.

Whether it was her words or that the sprites spied the crack, they sped ahead of us.

"Yours," Emily finished grandly, "for the taking."

She was supposed to finish "in reparation for the debt I owe you," but she'd started coughing, and by then the sprites were already in the cavern anyway.

Once again, Emily hugged my arms while I hugged her as hard as I could.

Let it work, let it work, let it work, I thought, alarmed by the way I could feel the erratic thumping of her heart.

There was a delighted squeal from the sprites—obviously, they'd spotted the gold. This was followed by an outraged roar from the dragon, who likewise had spotted the sprites. Next came by an angry shriek from the sprites, who'd become aware of the dragon. In a moment, dragon smoke aglitter with sprite sparkle billowed out of the crack.

Emily couldn't catch her breath and was coughing so hard she sounded on the verge of gagging, and now she was bent over with her hands pressed against her chest. "Ow," she moaned between those body-wrenching coughs.

I became aware that there were more sparkles in the air than could be attributed to the dragon-fighting sprites. The Land of the Golden Butterflies was dissolving.

But the question was: around both of us—or just around me?

Because in this world, I couldn't count on anything.

CHAPTER 25

End Game

M OM WAS LYING across Emily's couch sobbing, and I thought, *All that for nothing.*

So what that I had succeeded? I'd been about five seconds too late for Emily.

My sister was gone.

Not fair, not fair, not fair.

But I remembered someone—Mom, come to think of it—reproving me on my tenth birthday when I'd complained *no fair* that it was raining when we were supposed to be going to Darien Lake. Mom had snorted and said, *Since when is life fair, cupcake?*

Now, Mom pulled herself away from Emily's couch and flung herself on mine, and it was only then that I realized, yes, Mom was sobbing, but she was also laughing. And over her shoulder, I could see Emily, not ready to sit up yet, but awake, and smiling, and waving at me.

The first few minutes back at Rasmussem were wild.

Mom was doing her best to hug both of us, which was

a stretch, seeing as how Emily and I were on different couches.

Ms. Bennett was at the console, her fingers a blur of movement—I'm guessing shutting the Land of the Golden Butterflies program down quick, just in case Emily changed her mind and tried to go back in.

I felt so drained that I needed to set my head back down on the pillow while Mom was busy telling Emily—for the fourth or fifth time—"It's okay, honey, we'll work things out, everything's going to be fine."

It took a while before I became aware that Adam was standing beside my couch, holding Mom's phone out to me.

Without the energy to ask who it was, I took the phone and mumbled, "Hello?"

"Grace!" My dad's voice cracked. "Are you truly all right?"

"Yeah," I said, forcing more energy into my tone so Dad wouldn't sound so worried. "Emily and I are both fine." Then, my quick mind having already run out of anything useful to say, I added the obvious, "You finally got out of your meeting."

Dad took that as criticism. "I'm so sorry I wasn't there for you."

There were a few seconds of muddled conversation while we talked over each other, with me saying, "No, I didn't mean . . . ," and him saying, "Yeah, but I should . . . ," and we both said, "What?" and we both tried to repeat what we'd just said earlier; then we both stopped entirely.

After a few seconds of silence, Dad said, "The young man there told me you were the hero who saved the day."

I glanced at Adam, who had moved to help Ms. Bennett and had his back to me.

Hero? That's quite an upgrade for someone who's just come to terms with *levelheaded.*

"Well," I said, "that's a bit of an exaggeration . . ."

"No," Dad insisted, "he said you wouldn't give up, that you kept trying, no matter what. Grace, I'm so proud of you—and so grateful."

Well, so that was the good part.

The okay part was when Mr. Kroll, representing Rasmussem's legal department, came in. Mr. Kroll welcomed Emily back, with all his usual warmth and sincerity; he followed that with at least a half-hour of legalese, all of which came down to: *You don't sue us and we won't sue you.*

Oh, and by the way, pack up your stuff and don't bother thinking you'll ever work for Rasmussem again.

Working for Rasmussem had been Emily's dream for, like, forever, but all right, that was to be expected.

Then came the bad part.

I don't know about Mom, Dad, and Emily, but I'd assumed that once Emily made a formal statement about how she'd fiddled with the scores of those SAT tests, and once she'd apologized and promised never to do it again, she'd be forgiven. Maybe get a good talking-to from the people who run the SATs, maybe have a fine imposed by her college or even by the other colleges, the ones her friends had gotten into under false pretexts.

I was not expecting the police to come, to arrest her for fraud, and to take her away in handcuffs.

Thus began our education in the American judicial system. Before then, my family's sole experience in legal matters was that time my father had been to traffic court to contest a speeding ticket. So it's been a crash course in bail bondsmen, grand jury indictments, and endless hearings separated by interminable delays.

Our family has a lawyer now, not Mr. Kroll, of course, but a lawyer to look out for our interests, a lawyer our parents had to hire—and pay and pay and pay for. This lawyer of ours says Emily has two things on her side: her age and her obvious remorse. By sheerest luck, Emily was a couple of weeks short of her eighteenth birthday when she hacked into the computer system, making her a minor during the actual commission of the crime. Along with her attempted suicide (now that it's all over, we can acknowledge this), her confession, and her contrition, that makes a certain amount of leniency possible. Or so says our lawyer. He asserts his doubt that Emily will actually have to serve jail time. But then he admits she might.

Meanwhile, her high school friends, the ones whose

scores she padded, have each and every one of them been thrown out of the colleges they were attending. They'll need to retake the tests and apply—elsewhere, they've been told—next semester. Scholarship money had to be returned. In the case of Frank Lupiano, this was such a significant amount that his parents have had to take out a second mortgage on their house, their only option for keeping *him* out of jail.

Because of this, our family also got an education in hate mail and obscene phone calls. We've all had to change our e-mail accounts and phone numbers and social networking to avoid those former friends and their parents—and also to avoid people we don't even know, people who feel they lost the chance to go to the colleges they are sure they would otherwise have gotten into, if only Emily's friends hadn't wrongfully taken their places.

The first few weeks, Mom and Dad fluttered and hovered over Emily, always trying to keep a discreet watch on her, obviously worried that she would seek another way to escape her complicated life.

But actually . . . Emily . . . I don't know how to say this in a way that won't make those who hate my sister hate her more, but she is doing well. Sure, she's worried about her upcoming court date, about the sorrow she's caused, about how her actions have cut down so many of her options for the future. But even with all those fears and regrets, now that everything's gone public, now that she's no longer keeping secrets, it's like the worst is over. Our family has survived, and sometimes—not often, but sometimes—Emily even looks happy.

Not that I would ever wish what we went through on anybody else, but our relationship has evolved. It's not so much one of older sister/younger sister, but more one of longtime friends who have gone through a lot together. And I like that.

Mom is calmer, Dad is home more often, and my friends aren't interested in college yet—so they all think that Emily is kind of cool and that I am the Empress of the Total Immersion Universe. Sub-teen Games division, of course.

So what I'm saying is that I, too, am generally happy.

And I felt that even before Ms. Bennett texted me—clever computer engineer that she is, she somehow tracked down my new phone number. What she said was:

You did well.
Call me in another 5 years.

Not bad for the other sister, the levelheaded one—who still hates trigonometry.